Felicity stared at the pink cross—just stared at it for ever—telling herself she must have mixed the specimens up. But that argument failed in a trice—she was meticulous at that type of thing.

She couldn't be pregnant!

Couldn't be having Karim's baby…

There was no comfort in that thought, no sweet feeling of peace or surge of maternal protection—her only thought was one of unadulterated fear.

Two weeks ago she'd never even met him.

Two weeks ago she'd been a virgin.

She stared down at the pink cross again and the unpalatable truth hit her.

Yes, she was pregnant.

Pregnant by Sheikh Prince Karim of Zaraq.

BILLIONAIRE DOCTORS

*Hot, jet-set docs at the top of their game—
professionally...and personally!*

These desirable doctors are international
playboys—Gorgeous Greeks, sexy sheikhs,
irresistible Italians and Australian tycoons.

Their playground might be the world
of the rich and famous, but their
professional reputations are world renowned.

These billionaires dedicate themselves
to saving lives by day—
and red-hot seduction by night...

SECRET SHEIKH, SECRET BABY

BY
CAROL MARINELLI

MILLS & BOON

First published in Great Britain 2009
Large Print edition 2010
Harlequin Mills & Boon Limited,
Eton House, 18-24 Paradise Road,
Richmond, Surrey TW9 1SR

© Carol Marinelli 2009

ISBN: 978 0 263 21071 2

Harlequin Mills & Boon policy is to use papers that are
natural, renewable and recyclable products and made
from wood grown in sustainable forests. The logging and
manufacturing process conform to the legal environmental
regulations of the country of origin.

Printed and bound in Great Britain
by CPI Antony Rowe, Chippenham, Wiltshire

SECRET SHEIKH,
SECRET BABY

Carol Marinelli recently filled in a form where she was asked for her job title, and was thrilled, after all these years, to be able to put down her answer as writer. Then it asked what Carol did for relaxation. After chewing her pen for a moment, Carol put down the truth—writing. The third question asked—What are your hobbies? Well, not wanting to look obsessed or, worse still, boring, she crossed the fingers on her free hand and answered swimming and tennis. But, given that the chlorine in the pool does terrible things to her highlights, and the closest she's got to a tennis racket in the last couple of years is watching the Australian Open, I'm sure you can guess the real answer!

Recent titles by the same author:

Medical™ Romance:

A DOCTOR, A NURSE: A LITTLE MIRACLE
BILLIONAIRE DOCTOR, ORDINARY NURSE*
ENGLISH DOCTOR, ITALIAN BRIDE

Modern™ Romance:

HIRED: THE ITALIAN'S CONVENIENT MISTRESS
ITALIAN BOSS, RUTHLESS REVENGE
EXPECTING HIS LOVE-CHILD*

The House of Kolovsky

CHAPTER ONE

THE hotel was stunning.

Dashing through the luxurious foyer, Felicity Anderson would have loved to pause and take in her surroundings—or even, given that she had been caught in the rain on her dash from the London underground, race to the ladies' room and fix her hair and make-up. Her long, wavy blonde hair was tied back, and had early this morning been tamed with hair serum, but the run in the rain from the underground station would have undone all her hard work. There just wasn't time to worry about it. The information session started at ten a.m., and, glancing at her watch, Felicity grimaced because it was already a quarter past. Meticulous and punctual, she had arranged to arrive at nine and linger in a café beforehand, but track works had caused 'unexpected delays' on her train from the north of England, which meant that Felicity was, whether she liked it or not, unforgivably late.

The concierge had pointed her in the right direction for the conference room, and Felicity followed the discreet signs until she found the venue. There a pretty woman who introduced herself as Noor was sitting at the desk outside, and waved away Felicity's apologies.

'We are just glad that you made it.' Noor had thick, long, dark hair that was no doubt rather more neatly tied back than Felicity's. She was wearing an immaculate navy trouser suit, and her manicured hands held out a pen as she asked Felicity to sign the attendance register. 'On now is the introductory presentation about the hospital and the imminent opening of the university.' The dark-haired beauty handed Felicity a heavy bag which contained brochures and forms. 'You can look through them all later—come, I will take you through. Just stand at the back till the presentation ends, and then take a seat. We really are so pleased to see you, Felicity, and delighted that you are considering us. Zaraqua Hospital urgently needs good midwives.'

Felicity was just a little taken back by the warmth of Noor's welcome. But then all her dealings with Zaraqua Hospital had been pleasant. She felt a little bit guilty too—though she *had* explained that she already had a job in the Middle East lined up, bar signing on the dotted line, and was coming to the recruitment information session only out of last-minute curiosity. As a qualified midwife she knew her skills were in heavy demand, and she wanted to be sure she was making the right choice, but really her decision was almost made.

The room was in darkness, just illuminated

by the light of the vast screen as Felicity slipped in. Standing quietly, she watched the presentation, her decision wavering as she saw the stunning golden beaches of the Mediterranean sea that gave way to vast, vast desert. The Kingdom of Zaraq was an island with its own royal family, Felicity learnt, and its own deep traditions, though it was progressive too. An all-female university was opening, so the new generation of Zaraq women wouldn't have to leave the island and go overseas to be afforded first-class education. The fact that the university was an all-female environment appeased the more traditional families.

The information about the university was riveting to listen to, but it was the hospital Felicity was especially interested in. Her attention was utterly focussed as she was led through the lavish corridors, glimpsing plush suites, and her eyes widened as the impressive equipment and facilities were listed—this healthcare was available to *all* the people of Zaraq.

So focussed was Felicity that at first she barely registered the person who quietly came in. But as he stood beside her she knew that it was a man without turning her head. A delicious scent reached her nostrils, but more than that there was a presence, an all-male presence, that dragged her attention from the screen. Felicity turned her head and nodded an acknowledgment to the man. But then she couldn't, or didn't, immediately turn her face away.

Even in darkness his beauty was evident. Instead of leaning against the wall, as Felicity was, he stood to an impressive height. His hair was cropped close to his head, and she saw sculpted features, a straight nose, and deep shadows beneath his cheekbones, and eyes that in the darkness momentarily held hers. He gave a brief nod and she jerked her eyes away, turned her supposed attention back to the screen. She felt as if her face were on fire. She held her head rigid and did not allow herself to follow instinct and turn again to look at him.

His presence was devastating—completely overwhelming. It wasn't just his scent, it wasn't just his looks, it was *something* that consumed her as she stood. She had travelled for hours to be here, to learn about the hospital and nursing roles on the island of Zaraq. She had come here so she could make a wise and informed choice. Yet it might as well have been a cartoon on the screen for all the attention she was paying it. He was well over a metre away and yet it felt as if he were right next to her, touching her almost. The darkness was intimate, and she knew—just knew—he had turned his head to her again and was looking at her. She could hardly breathe, hardly swallow, grateful for the wall that was behind her holding her up.

Not once had she felt like this.

Even her ex-boyfriend Paul's most tender administration of affection hadn't elicited even a quarter of this response—their relationship had in fact broken up because of it. Felicity was unable, *physically* unable, to give that piece of herself—and yet, here in the darkness that piece of her she had searched for, the elusive *thing* that every other human on earth seemed to possess, had emerged. Like a shoot after the cold soil of winter, she felt a stir of warmth, the split of a seed, a surfacing that here in the darkness felt surreal.

She was going mad.

Staring at the screen, trying to concentrate, trying to slow her breathing, Felicity thought she was, right there and then, going completely insane. For a full year she'd seen a psychologist along with Paul—had also been to a gynaecologist who had broken her hymen and given her a strange set of dilators to gradually get her body used to the idea. But nothing—not endless warm bubble baths, nor

Paul taking it slowly, not a tranquiliser or a glass of wine, nor a plea to 'just please do it' had worked.

Nothing.

Yet here, standing in the darkness, feeling his eyes on her, smelling *him*, sensing *him*, had he walked that short distance over and pressed his face onto hers she would have kissed him. She could almost imagine him pushing into her. Her panties were damp just from standing there near him. *How* would it be if he were closer?

And then he was gone.

He just slipped quietly away. A chink of light showed from the door as he made his exit, and finally Felicity could breathe again. She stood for a moment and collected herself before the room was flooded in light, and then she slipped into a seat, her mind, her body still whirring.

'You didn't miss much!' A friendly face smiled, and the man introduced himself as Liam Edwards.

'Just the first fifteen minutes,' Felicity lied—because thanks to the mystery man she'd practically missed all of the introductory presentation.

'Lucky you!' Liam rolled his eyes. 'It was all about the royal family and King Zaraq and his sons. Still, the hospital looks fantastic. I'm a nurse, by the way. I work in emergency,' he added, 'and me and my girlfriend are trying to save for a deposit for a house. This looks like a good way. She's an emergency nurse too. What about you?'

'I'm a midwife.' Felicity's smile was fixed. She wished she'd chosen another seat, not next to this chatty stranger. She was glad when Noor stepped on stage and introduced the first speaker, Judith Lansdon, a woman in her fifties, who was a professor of medicine and in charge of the medical faculty at the university.

Though the professor's talk was no doubt fascinating, Felicity had to force herself to concentrate, still reeling from what had just occurred. Then she asked herself *what* had occurred? She had nothing with which to compare it.

'Now, a few facts about Zaraq before your various specialities are addressed,' the host announced. 'The new all-female university is something we are very proud of on the island. The university has been built beside the hospital in the main city of Zaraqua, which is set near the ocean. Most of Zaraq is inhospitable desert—yet the island has its own economy, its own airport and a thriving tourist industry with stunning seven-star resorts. The compound attached to the university and the hospital where you would be living has every luxury. But be aware that Zaraq holds dear its traditions. Though this is a progressive monarchy, it has its own rules—rules that are outlined in the guidelines you have been given. They are non-negotiable. I strongly suggest that you read them carefully before you consider embarking on this journey. Sheikh King Kaliq Zaraq insists on good healthcare for all his subjects. In fact it is hoped at some time in the future to implement an outreach programme for the Bedouin people, though this is a sensitive area.'

The morning wore on, and gradually the strange encounter faded a touch from her thoughts as Felicity's well-laid plans started to change. Each speaker had her more and more impressed, and with each hour that passed her decision became harder. She had arranged to go to the Middle East for two years to nurse, and her paperwork had been approved, and she was just a couple of days away from signing her contract. But one day her attention had been caught by an article about the new university in Zaraq, and she had looked it up on the internet. She had seen an amazing state-of-the-art maternity hospital. On a last-minute impulse Felicity had rung the information number. On hearing she was a qualified midwife, they had invited her to attend today, and now Felicity, as they all trooped out for a sumptuous buffet lunch, was torn with indecision. Should she just stay with the hospital she had first chosen, or start the process all over again so that she could nurse in Zaraq?

'What do you think?' Liam asked as they stood chatting through lunch. 'The pay's better than at the other hospitals…'

'It looks very impressive. I think it might well be a yes.' Felicity nodded. 'I just hope it doesn't take too long. I'll have to find out more about the application procedure.' She didn't add that her family was desperate for the money this work would bring in. After years of seeing her sister struggle with a severe eating disorder Felicity had taken a vast loan, and Georgie's problems had finally been properly addressed in a top private clinic. Though Felicity considered the money well spent, the fact was, it was money she didn't have. Now it was time to pay it back.

She did not share this information with Liam—not that it stopped him from divulging what was on *his* mind.

'My girlfriend and I will have to get married if we go.' He didn't look too pleased at the idea.

'That's not just in Zaraq.' Felicity frowned. 'If you want to live together in most parts of the Middle East you have to be married. Have you done any research at all?'

'This is it!' Liam shrugged and carried on chatting, but Felicity was lost again. Midway to putting a small, perfectly cut sandwich to her lips, she saw him—across the room, talking to Noor. Worse, he was looking at her, and in the light he was better than beautiful, he was utterly stunning. He had a rakish, haughty face, full, sensual lips—and in four split seconds Felicity achieved more insight into her sister Georgie's eating disorder than she had in all her research and education.

The most natural thing was to carry on, to chat to Liam, to eat the tiny sliver of bread. But she was so supremely self-conscious, so awkward, so aware of her mouth, her teeth as they bit in, her tongue, her jaw as she chewed, her throat as she swallowed, she gave in, put the loaded plate down, and settled for water instead.

Who the hell *was* he?

It was a question that would remain unanswered. Through the afternoon lectures, despite her eyes scanning the room for him, despite feeling as if she were on high alert waiting for him to reappear, there was no further sign of him. When the session ended at five p.m. it was with a certain reluctance that she accepted she would never see him again. Her mystery man would remain just that—a mystery.

'See you.' Liam grinned, rushing past as she lingered in the foyer. 'But not in Zaraq!'

Felicity laughed. 'Not for you then?'

'Nope. Do you want to grab a coffee?' he offered, but though she would have loved to linger a little while longer, to catch one final glimpse of *him*, her train left in twenty minutes. If she missed that one then she'd miss her connection, and she wouldn't make it back home tonight. Felicity declined, smiling. As she walked through to Reception she could see the grey London streets and the rain threatening. She rummaged in her bag for her small umbrella and heard her phone bleeping.

'Hi, Mum!'

'How was it?'

'Great.' Felicity smiled. 'Too good actually. Now I think I want to go to Zaraq.'

'Well, you're not going anywhere tonight...'

Felicity groaned as her mother continued.

'I looked up the trains and there's been some trouble on the line. No service till tomorrow. There is a bus, apparently, but it only takes you halfway and you have to change.'

'It will take *hours*.' There was no chance of her getting home before midnight at this rate.

'What are you going to do?'

'Don't worry.' Felicity could hear her mother getting anxious, and as always moved quickly to quash it. 'I'll be fine; I can stay in London overnight.'

'But you haven't booked in anywhere. You don't know anyone!'

'Mum, I'm twenty-six,' Felicity interrupted calmly. 'I'm more than capable of surviving a night in London.'

Her credit card wasn't, though!

Still, as Felicity turned off her phone she was suddenly glad of the train cancellation. The thought of a night to herself was rather tempting—it had been way too long since she'd had one. Her time recently had been taken up with visiting her sister in the eating disorder unit, or stopping by at her mum's for a little pep-talk. Even since Georgie's discharge she hadn't been able to relax, with her mother or sister ringing almost constantly. Then there was taking Georgie to out-patients' appointments, and trying to work overtime as the never-ending medical bills and loan repayments rapidly caught up.

It would be nice to have a night alone.

A night when for once Felicity Anderson could just be that.

Not midwife, not daughter, not sister, not carer, not provider.

Just plain old Felicity would do very nicely.

Karim liked London.

He was an occasional visitor, though recently he had been coming a lot more often. He had been overseeing the recruitment process for his hospital and university, as well as visiting his mother and checking on several investments and businesses he had stakes in. He wasn't busy enough though for his liking—not in the way he was in Zaraq, or had been. Karim blew out a long breath.

It was hard to get excited about million-dollar deals when they were but a drop in the ocean of his family's vast wealth. Hard too to inject enthusiasm into the recruitment process. The hospital and the university had been his inception, both ideas had fired him up at the time—but Karim didn't want to be watching films or looking at brochures of well-equipped hospitals. He wanted to be working in one. He wanted to stretch his brilliant mind with a complicated diagnosis, or to immerse himself fully in a long operation. But thanks to his status those opportunities were getting fewer and further between.

Still, he loved the relative anonymity London gave him. Here, though he worked seemingly hard, there was no real responsibility. Here he was carefree—a playboy prince who regularly indulged. It was so very different from his rigid, high-profile life back home. Here he could walk the streets unrecognised—which his security team hated him doing more than anything. Karim refused to bend. Dressed in a dark suit with a full-length overcoat he actually enjoyed the rain, enjoyed the changing seasons he witnessed when he came here. Late autumn was a season he liked, perhaps the most. This weekend he would drive to the country, get out of the city...

As his phone bleeped he gave it a cursory glance and then rolled his eyes. It was Leila again—he would have his aide, Khan, speak with her and forbid her from pestering him.

Yes, he would drive to the country—and, he decided, he would not go alone...

Karim thought only briefly of the rather difficult conversation he had had with Leila earlier this week, telling his long-term mistress that her services were no longer required. She hadn't taken it at all well—but then, what woman ever did?

Karim enjoyed and had bedded many women, though he believed absolutely in monogamy. After all, he always ensured the fling, or relationship, or whatever it was called, was confirmed as over before he readily moved on to the next! But not for much longer. He was being pushed further and further towards marriage by his father—

something Karim was doing his best to avoid. Leila had delusions of grandeur—had thought that their three-month fling might be leading somewhere—and was refusing to listen now Karim had told her that marriage to her was not and never had been his intention. Over the past two weeks she had become demanding. When Karim didn't take her calls she would pester his aides—and, most importantly to Karim, the sex hadn't been that good!

Well, it had been good, Karim corrected—it had just taken too long! He was a marvellous lover—he had no issues there—and he lavished his lovers with attention. He did all the right things, and they certainly wept for more. It was really a time issue. With an appetite as insatiable as Karim's sometimes there simply wasn't *time*, and Leila had been insisting recently on the full theatre, when for Karim sometimes all he needed was her mouth.

Enough, he had decided. It was over and he had dealt with it—to his father's dismay. His father had told Karim in no uncertain terms that it was time now to find a bride—which was why he'd flown to London. For one last play, one last feast of indulgence, before duty caught up and he married a suitable bride.

When he had slipped into the meeting room and been greeted by that stunning blonde he had felt the attraction—*how* he had felt it. And at lunchtime he had been sorely tempted to walk over. Still, when Noor had explained she was there to consider working in the maternity section of the hospital, Karim had decided it might be rather messy should he see her at work. He had decided that an afternoon stroll might be safer, so he'd rung Mandy, whose eyes weren't quite as blue and whose hair wasn't naturally blonde, and arranged to see her tonight. Even if she wasn't *her*, Karim was blessed with a good imagination—if he could stop Mandy talking for half an hour he would have a good night!

He'd headed back to the hotel only once the

information session was over—happy with himself until he saw the real thing, walking out of the hotel and looking straight towards him.

Karim smiled and walked towards her. Why should he settle for a poor imitation?

It had been raining, Felicity realised, and it was about to seriously pour again. The sky was heavy and dark, the streets wet and un-inviting. And then she saw him, walking towards her, dressed in a long black coat. With his dark hair he should have blended in with the rest, but he stood out, luminous almost in the grey and gloomy day.

And he saw her looking.

The underground was across the street and to the left. There was a moment for Felicity—a mysterious, inexplicable moment—when she knew she could walk down the steps and turn left, could turn her back and that would be it; or she could stand still and see what happened.

It was bizarre, watching as the rain started

to fall, as everyone else hastened their speed or paused and put up umbrellas. His stride never changed. He just walked towards her with purpose in his eyes—determination, almost—and with a stab of regret she knew that it was pointless. Even if he engineered a conversation, asked her to join him for coffee or dinner, even if he was as stunning to talk to as he was to look at, all she would do in the long run was disappoint.

Mission pointless, Felicity realised, shaking herself out of her momentary trance, and she went down the steps and turned left.

There was Liam, walking out of a coffee shop over the road with a large muffin in his hand. Everybody was going back to their lives, and so too must she. As she pushed the traffic light button her head was whirring, trying to define what it was she had turned her back on—because not a word between them had been said.

The lights were changing, cars, taxis, cyclists and buses all slowing down and the green light was about to flash to tell the pedestrians to walk. She almost *wanted* his hand to come on her shoulder, for this mysterious man to haul her back to his world.

There was no hand on her shoulder. It was self-preservation that caused her to step back. In fact Felicity pulled an elderly lady back too, as she saw that one car wasn't slowing down—if anything it was speeding up. In the small amount of time it took for it happen, Felicity saw everything. The female driver, her head back, jerking at the wheel, the slide of the car over the crossing, and the horrific sound of a revved engine. It was like a missile turning and randomly choosing its course. It could have ended up anywhere—on the crowded pavement, in a packed café window. With no time to move, to register, even to run, an eerie silence descended. And then came a ripping sound of metal that went on for ever, a thud of impact as the small car slammed into a bus, its wheels still scratching and spinning, its engine still revving.

Then people moved.

The chance of an explosion was imminent.

As the crowd scattered, a few people ran forward.

Felicity could see the hotel doorman and Liam, running towards the centre of the bus, pulling on the closed doors. *He* was running too—but to the crashed car, as was she.

'She was fitting,' Felicity called out to him. He was leaning in the car as she sped over, her smart high heels hard work in the rain. She realised she hadn't been heard above the scream of the engine as she reached him, and shouted again. 'She was fitting!'

He had reached in and turned off the engine, but still it was dangerous and he told her so. 'Get back—this could go up at any time.'

It was the first time she had heard his voice. Deep and accented, it was telling her very clearly to leave the scene. Liam was telling her the same, having helped off the passengers after he had dashed to the centre of the bus. Seeing just how dangerous it was, he told Felicity to get the hell out.

'They're all off the bus. Driver's got minor injuries. The fire engine will be here in a moment—it's unstable…'

It was—smoke was billowing from the car engine. Felicity could hear sirens in the background. Help was never far away on busy London streets—except the streets were packed, and the short distance between help and the accident was blocked with cars.

'Go!' *He* didn't turn to say it—he was supporting the woman's head; she was breathing but unconscious—but he made his orders clear. 'Get back *now*!'

So she did—albeit reluctantly. Felicity knew it was up to the experts, that if he chose to risk his life then that was his choice. And then she heard it, the shrieks of a newborn baby. Not fearful, stunned shrieks, but like those of a wounded animal, and she could no more walk away now than fly.

Liam was calling her back, telling her not to be foolish, but Felicity ignored him. *He*, the beautiful stranger, didn't question her decision as she approached. He was still holding the woman's head but he was also assessing the car for an opening, trying to locate the piercing screams of the baby. He didn't order her to leave again—knew perhaps he would be wasting his time—and time was of the essence.

Felicity wrenched at the crumpled car door and tried to get her head in the small gap she created.

'The baby's bleeding.' Though it was wrapped in a blue blanket, the little white baby suit was dark with blood on the arm. Felicity's head couldn't fit fully in, but she could see a shard of metal sticking out of the babe's arm, and even though the blood loss looked relatively small, for such a tiny infant it was substantial.

'There's a piece of metal…'

'Felicity.' She was surprised that he knew her name, but he said rapidly, 'I'm Karim. Can you get your arm in? Can you reach?'

She was already trying—only she couldn't see and stretch inside at the same time.

'I can't get in!'

'No.' His voice was calm and assured. 'Turn around and put your arm in that way. You will be able to reach; you will be able to hear me.'

'But I can't see.'

'I will guide you.' His voice was accented, rich and strong, and so assured, it reassured *her*. It made Felicity think that she could do it.

She had no choice *but* to do it.

One last glance at the baby to get her bearings showed her the patch of blood was spreading. She could see the shard of metal in its arm and knew she had to apply pressure.

She turned her head, the rain lashing her face as her arm slid into the dry confines of the car.

'Lower your hand,' Karim ordered. 'That is the base of the crib.'

Crib? The baby seat, Felicity translated to herself. He was holding the patient's head and ducking his own in and out of the vehicle, so that he could be her eyes on the inside and speak to her on the outside. Inch by inch her fingers crept forward.

'Now to your right. Feel his foot? That is his right foot. Move up.'

The injured arm was the baby's left one, and Felicity slowly moved her hand upwards with Karim's guidance. The baby had stopped screaming now, and was just making little noises—which was even more worrying than the crying. Without Karim's instruction her fingers located the sternum, the neck, and tried to move to the left.

'I can't reach,' Felicity said. 'I can't.'

'Two inches,' Karim said, and she was grateful then for her high heels—and for Karim urging her on. 'Careful,' Karim warned, but because she had seen, she knew where the metal was. She slipped her fingers into the babe's axilla and pushed upwards.

'Is it stopping?'

'I don't know,' Karim admitted. 'Just keep pushing.'

So she did.

For what felt like for ever.

The emergency services had arrived and the passenger door was peeled back a touch further. She could get her head inside now. She couldn't move to cover the baby with a blanket as the firefighter punched in the rear window—Karim did that. A paramedic had put a collar on the mother, and she had been extracted, but instead of stepping back, Karim climbed in further, covered the baby with an ambulance blanket, and covered Felicity's head too.

'She needs a hard hat,' a fire officer called.

'There's no room for a hard hat,' Karim responded. 'Turn your head,' Karim said to Felicity, which she did. Screwing her eyes closed, she tried not to move as the emergency crew created rear access to the baby.

And Karim stayed with her in the strange little tent.

He talked her through it, as her hand was numb and she wasn't sure if the baby was alive or dead.

'The firefighters have doused the engines,' he assured her. 'It shouldn't be much longer now.'

'My legs are freezing,' Felicity admitted.

'It will be over soon.' He held her eyes, black on blue, and it helped. She could hear the chatter of the firefighters and the paramedics behind her, but it was Karim's voice she was listening to. 'They are giving oxygen to him now.' It was as if he was her translator, and she could only listen to him, only trust what he was telling her, because he had been her eyes. 'They want to put IV access into his scalp before they move him. Can you hold on a little while more?'

Her whole arm and shoulder weren't only numb now, they hurt. Her body was trying not to shake, though she was frozen. She thought of all her mums in the last throes of labour, when it was all too much, when it was impossible, and yet still, with encouragement, somehow they pushed on.

'You *can* hold on,' Karim said, and she listened to him instead of to her body, that wanted to stop. She told herself it wasn't for much longer and pushed on.

'Got him.' A hand was over hers, pushing where she had, and a nameless voice told her she could let go now.

'Move her slowly backwards,' Karim ordered whoever was supporting her—because now she *could* let go Felicity was unsteady. She had to be pulled back rather than just remove herself from the car. Then she stood massaging her arm, tears pricking at her eyes as Karim climbed out too.

'Well done,' he said, and then changed his mind. 'I told you to get back. You should think before you rush in.'

'Did *you*?' Felicity commented.

'You should be more careful—there could have been more victims.'

What made the rules different for him? Felicity thought, and then winced as blood rushed back to her numb arm. She stared down at her soaked, filthy clothes. Her hair and face were drenched, and suddenly she didn't need scolding. She was close to crying, and he must have seen that because he changed tack.

'Go into the hotel,' Karim instructed. 'I will come and speak with you there.'

'I'm fine…' Felicity attempted, but gave in because clearly she wasn't—not that Karim was listening. His attention was back on the accident scene.

Felicity looked on. The world was coming back into focus now, as her circulation returned. The street was awash with fire trucks and paramedics. The little babe was being lifted out in his intact child seat, loads of hands gently guiding the little life to safety. It was like watching a baby being born—a long, silent pause, then relief from the crowd, from everyone, as he was safely delivered from the confines of the car. A blanket had been put around her shivering shoulders and Felicity just stood and took it all in. But not Karim. Even though there were doctors and paramedics, all waiting to assist, he didn't relinquish control. He snapped out orders as Felicity continued to stand and watch.

Just who *was* this man?

Only when the ambulance doors closed— when the siren blasted and the police directed it away—only then, when there was nothing more either could do, did he come over to Felicity and without a word guide her inside the hotel.

Just as she had known he would.

CHAPTER TWO

'WELL, I don't think we need to check your references!'

They were sitting in the sumptuous hotel lounge; Felicity had relinquished her blanket and was shivering as Karim rapidly ordered drinks. Piping hot chocolate appeared in a moment. Soaking wet and shivering, and completely out of place in such surroundings, she must have looked a sight—but because Karim didn't turn a hair, neither did she. For now.

He gave her a kind smile and it dawned on Felicity where she was—not her surroundings, more the company. She was sitting with the man who had captured her attention for the entire day—the man she had chosen at the last moment to avoid. Now here she was, sitting drinking hot chocolate, the sole focus of his attention.

And she had every right to be nervous!

Now that everyone had stopped looking at her, she was able to look at him—and he really was the most heart-stoppingly beautiful man she had ever seen. His coat had been removed by a waiter, and his gorgeous charcoal suit—apart from damp cuffs—was completely unscathed. His short black hair was glossy and wet, and his tie and the top of his shirt were loosened. He might have stepped out of a board meeting. The superbly cut suit accentuated his long limbs, and his olive complexion was set off with a crisp white shirt and gunmetal tie. His eyes were black, and they were kind, but they were not friendly. There was an elusive quality to him that Felicity couldn't quite put her finger on. An air of superiority that had Felicity fast realising that she hadn't a hope of relaxing and enjoying his company!

'Allow me to introduce myself—I am Karim. I oversee recruitment for the university and the hospital.'

Which was a rather vague introduction. Felicity frowned.

'You're a doctor?' she checked. He had known what he was doing out there, had retained control even when the emergency services had arrived. He was more than a recruitment consultant—of that she was sure.

'A surgeon.' Karim nodded. 'Though I rarely practise now. Recruitment is my focus.' He changed the subject. 'And you are Felicity Anderson, a fully qualified midwife who has all her paperwork up to date and is ready to leave.'

'How do you know?'

'Because I checked who you were with Noor.'

'Oh!' She blamed it on the hot chocolate, but she felt pink returning to her pale cheeks.

'I asked her to point out any midwives or emergency nurses. We are very short of both.'

'I see.' Felicity nodded. So that was why he

had been looking. She only had her imagination to blame for thinking otherwise.
Curiously deflated, she sat there, exhausted
now, as the adrenaline that had seen her
through the accident fully wore off.

'You did very well out there.' Karim
looked her over approvingly, but sadly,
Felicity realised, he was assessing only her
nursing skills. 'Without you the baby would
have exsanguinated.'

'I just hope I did enough soon enough.'

'I will ring and find out later,' Karim said,
looking forward to the prospect—perhaps
they could do that from his room! 'So, do you
live in London?'

'Unfortunately, no!'

'Unfortunately?' Karim checked.

'I live in the north, and my train just got
cancelled.' She was drained at the prospect of
finding somewhere to stay, but Karim clearly
thought he had the answer.

'Stay here tonight, then.'

'I don't think so!' She gave a small laugh; certainly she'd love to stay here—would love to peel off her damp, muddied clothes and climb into a fluffy white bathrobe rather than trudge the streets searching for accommodation that was rather more basic. But it was impossible, that was all! At that moment her phone rang. Not wanting to be rude, Felicity ignored it, and Karim gave a slight frown.

'It's my mum!' she said, by way of explanation.

'Shouldn't you speak with her?'

'I did a little while ago,' Felicity said, and then relented a touch. 'She suffers with anxiety. It's easier if I ring her when I've found out where I'm staying.'

'You just have,' Karim said. 'You will stay as our guest.'

'*Our* guest?'

'Zaraqua's guest!' He spoke as if the city was a person. 'We invited you to attend today's information session; now you have missed your train and you have also saved a baby's life. Of course it is our responsibility to ensure you get safely home. If that means you stay in London tonight, then so be it…'

'I couldn't possibly.' Felicity shook her head.

'This is how it will be.' Karim stood up. 'Excuse me for one moment.'

Felicity watched his broad back as he strode through the lounge. He really did have the most amazing presence. Every head turned as he walked past. She sat quietly, determinedly ignoring her phone, which was ringing again. She wished her mother would wait a little. Felicity *would* ring her, she resolved again, when she knew what was happening herself.

'Here.' Felicity jumped slightly and put down the scone she was eating as Karim returned and handed her a neat navy folder. 'It has all been arranged.'

It had too! She opened the folder, saw her room number and a swipe card, and could scarcely believe it. She was also just a little nervous as to what she was being offered. 'Are you sure?' Felicity frowned, completely unused to being spoilt, to things being sorted for her—normally that was *her* role. Still, the incident had shaken her up enough that she didn't have it in her to protest too much! 'Are you sure about this?'

'Absolutely.' Karim nodded. 'You cannot go home in wet clothes. Use the laundry service, and you have full use of the facilities—perhaps visit the spa... After today, you deserve to relax, And,' he added, 'may I say again well done. They are both very lucky that you were there.'

She deserved this, Karim thought. This woman who had just saved a life should not be stranded in London. She deserved to be spoiled, pampered. He insisted to himself he would have done the same for any attendee, but as he had arranged her accommodation he had shamelessly upgraded her—several notches, in fact. A rather confusing thought had occurred to him. Karim remembered the moment before the accident—the moment this woman had turned her back on him.

'Well, thank you,' Felicity said, retrieving her bag from the floor. 'It will be nice to get out of these clothes…' She stopped abruptly, a little embarrassed at her choice of words. 'Thank you again.'

She was going, Karim realised with a frown. Her words *had* been unintentional. There was no hint of flirting, no lingering to see if he might ask her to join him later…

'Would you like another drink?' Karim asked, but she shook her head.

'No, thanks.'

'Perhaps later?' When again she shook her head, Karim couldn't be bothered to pursue it. He was here in London for fun, and this was starting to feel like hard work.

As Felicity stood to go the waiter came over.

'Will you and your guest be dining with us tonight, Your…?'

He was frowned into silence. Karim had given strict instruction that his title was not to be used within the hotel—his security team were miserable enough with his jogging and walking the London streets, without alerting the public that there was a sheikh royal prince in their midst.

'Sir!' The waiter changed his words with a cough.

Karim was about to decline. He thought of Mandy, ever ready and waiting, and then looked to where Felicity stood. Her face was blushing scarlet, her eyes so startled he half expected her to turn and run. Maybe he should just let her. But he remembered again the attraction that had flared in the presentation room, that unacknowledged arousal between them that had rendered him so hard he had had to get out. He decided the effort might be worth it—he wanted to go there again.

'Would you like to join me?'

He saw the dart of her eyes, and—always

smooth, always polite—said the right thing. 'Forgive me—that was crass. Of course you do not have to join me. There is no obligation.'

'I know…' Felicity managed a small laugh as he voiced her urgent thoughts and then checked herself. Her accommodation was sorted, and now the most impossibly attractive man was asking her for dinner… So what if it couldn't lead to anything? So what if there was no point in pursuing a romance with this man? She hadn't had a night out or off in months.

Staring into his black eyes, at that moment the answer was easy. 'I'd love to join you, except…' She gestured to her crumpled and soaked linen suit.

'The hotel will sort that…' He waved his hand as if it *were* that easy. 'And I can give you an update on the mother and baby over dinner.'

'Thank you.' Felicity nodded.

'We will meet at eight,' Karim said. 'Here?'

'That would be lovely.'

* * *

It *would* be lovely, Felicity thought as Karim stalked out of the hotel lounge. But, glancing at her watch, she realised she had only just over an hour to prepare! So, after ringing her mother to tell her a rather loose version of her plans, Felicity snapped into urgent mode and dashed to a chemist. She bought some stockings, a toothbrush and paste, and some hair serum, and then went up to her room.

Only it wasn't a room—it was a suite. A vast sprawling suite, with flowers and chocolates and even a bucket of champagne cooling in a silver bucket.

And then someone knocked at the door.

Her heart stilled. She was nervous that it was Karim, that she had misinterpreted the exceptionally friendly gesture after all.

But it was a woman with an instant wardrobe on a trolley, that she wheeled into Felicity's room. Felicity just stood there as she was informed to help herself, and told that her own clothes would be laundered and back to her by morning.

She couldn't get her head around it. She was used—too used—to being two steps ahead of everything, to being the one who anticipated problems, the one who sorted things out. Yet since she had stepped into the hotel—since her first greeting from Noor—she had been looked after, her needs anticipated, and she had been rewarded for a job well done too.

It felt nice.

Unfamiliar, but very, *very* nice.

Peeling off her damp clothes, Felicity took in her suite.

It had everything—and she hadn't needed to worry about the toothpaste and brush. The little basket of goodies in the bathroom contained everything a girl might need, Felicity thought as she found a teeny pump bottle of hair serum. And even things a girl didn't need too…

Like condoms!

Oh, Karim had assured her there were no obligations, but that wasn't why she dropped them like a hot coal. Whatever Karim might be expecting from her, it was never going to happen.

Felicity sat, deflated, on the edge of the huge oval bath and stared at herself in the mirror.

Her blonde hair was tumbled, there was still a flush of excitement in her cheeks, and her blue eyes were glittering at the prospect of dinner with Karim. But, as Paul had found out, dinner was all it would ever be. What if tonight went well? Felicity worried. What if he asked to see her again? And what if they went out for a few weeks…? She screwed her eyes closed at the prospect. At what point did you tell someone? She knew it was impossible for them to have a relationship, knew it was pointless to pursue it, but she *did* want dinner with him…

And dinner was all it could ever be for her— even with a man as dashing as Karim.

CHAPTER THREE

HE WAS waiting for her.

Karim stood as she walked into the hotel lounge, and his decision as to his choice of date for the night was instantly confirmed as the right one.

She was wearing a pale grey woollen dress, a modest dress—yet it clung nicely to her trim waist, and Karim noticed the scooped neckline. It accentuated her full bust...

He had idly wondered what she would achieve in an hour. Used to summoning mistresses, he had women on tap and permanently ready. This one was not used to his ways, and yet she had done exceptionally well! No one would possibly guess that just a short while ago she had been saving a life in the driving rain.

Her hair, that had been tied back in all of the short time he had known her, was loose now. Soft and newly washed, it fell over her shoulders. Her long, slim legs were encased in stockings, her feet in dark grey stilettos.

Yes, he was glad of his choice of company for the night. But as he placed his hand on her elbow and guided her through the restaurant, and she shot forward at the slight contact, he knew it was going to be a long one! Unashamedly he had checked her CV. He knew that she was twenty-six and single, yet she was acting like a gauche teenager on her first date.

Oh, well, Karim decided glancing at his watch. If they weren't in bed by eleven he could be at Mandy's by twelve!

He'd give her three hours!

The menu was impossible. Oh, there was plenty that at first glance she liked, but sitting opposite Karim made the simplest decision impossible. He was wearing a different suit, had used his hour to shower and change too. Felicity could see that—and smell it. She was somewhat relieved and a little irritated too when his phone rang. He answered it, and after a brief apology spoke to whoever was on the line in rapid Arabic.

'I am sorry about that.' He put his phone down, and then picked it up again and turned it off. 'That was an old friend and colleague of mine. He is working at the hospital the casualties were taken to—he always speaks in our own language.'

'How are they?' Felicity asked, glad now that he had taken the call, but worried as to what she might hear.

'The mother has regained consciousness. She had another seizure on arrival, but she is doing well.'

'And the baby?'

'Is in Theatre now,' Karim said. 'It will take a while, but the surgeons are very hopeful.'

'Did he regain consciousness?'

'Yes!' Karim nodded. 'They resuscitated with fluids. There is one problem...' He paused for just a moment and Felicity held her breath. 'He's a *she*!'

'Oh!' Felicity blinked, remembering the blue blanket. 'Well, there's a reminder never to assume!' She smiled, and he did too. He had lovely white even teeth, with just a tiny irregularity. But even that made him more exquisite; this was no capped, manufactured smile, and he really was, as she had first realised, devastating.

With only brief consultation he took care of the wine and the ordering, and was such pleasant company that by the time she had struggled through the entrée and moved onto the main Felicity was almost able to relax.

But not fully—because always, *always* her mind was on the end of night, or the next night, or the next.

This *was* a date.

A real one.

And real ones—good ones—led to more dates…

'You may find things different in Zaraqua,' Karim warned her, after he had pressed her about her work and she had told him how she was a strong advocate for natural childbirth with minimum intervention. 'We have top-class facilities and equipment, and we do tend to use them.'

'I have thought about that,' Felicity said, 'and I'm not looking to change the world. I work in a low-risk birthing centre at the moment— hopefully I'll come away from Zaraq more informed, which can only be good.'

'You have an open mind.' Karim smiled. 'You would not make a good surgeon.'

'I'm a good midwife, though,' Felicity said, and smiled back.

'Did you tell your mother you were staying here?'

'No!' Felicity said. 'I just told her I had found

somewhere.' She saw his slight frown. 'She'd only worry more if I told her about the crash.'

'It must be hard, having a parent who worries so.'

'It is,' Felicity admitted, and thanked the waiter as her main course was taken away. 'And I'm still not sure if I'm doing the right thing, going overseas. My sister hasn't been well for a couple of years,' she explained. 'She's doing fine now, but there have been a lot of expenses. This way I can really tackle them. Only…' She hesitated. The practical solution she had come up with for her family had been a sensible one, but there was an emotional side to it too—one she had never shared and certainly not with a stranger.

'Only…?' Karim checked.

'I'm not sure I'm doing the right thing—I'm not sure how they'll manage. Georgie, my sister, has an eating disorder. She's doing brilliantly now, though.' She swallowed uncomfortably, nervous of voicing her innermost fears. 'I'm just worried that my leaving will set her back. But I don't really have a choice.'

'Georgie has,' Karim said as a white chocolate mousse drizzled in hot raspberry sauce was placed in front of her. 'She can choose to stay well or not—you cannot do that for her.'

He was right—of course he was right—only it wasn't so straightforward.

'You don't understand…'

'I can assure you I do!' Karim responded. 'I know all there is to know about duty and family. And I know how it feels to be the strong one.'

Karim had declined dessert, and was working his way through a cheese platter. Now her dessert bowl was empty, it merited just a little look from her. He pushed the platter forward and, to her own surprise, instead of refusing and saying she was fine, Felicity took a cracker and helped herself.

'What about your father?' Karim asked, watching as the cracker paused midway to her mouth.

'He died a few years ago.'

'I'm sorry. That must have been hard for you all.'

She stared across the table at him, stared into black, assessing eyes that gave absolutely nothing away—eyes that judged but were somehow not judging. Instead of taking the easy option and accepting his condolences, after a brief hesitation she responded.

'Don't be sorry. He caused this mess. What about *your* family?'

He gave a brief shrug. 'There is not much to tell.'

'Oh?'

He stabbed a piece of cheese with his knife and smeared it on some bread, then took a sliver of quince jelly and topped it with that. He handed it to her and then did the same for himself.

Karim never usually shared—he was generous with gifts, he just never shared what was his.

But tonight he did.

'I have two brothers. My mother lives here in London—my father is in Zaraq.'

'Are they divorced?' For a second she was sure his face tightened, and she thought she must have said the wrong thing. It was an entirely natural assumption—just the wrong one.

'There is no divorce in Zaraq. My mother, even though she lives in England, gave my father four sons. She deserves his support and respect.'

This was a rather different way of looking at things than Felicity was used to hearing in the maternity wards! But he'd confused her now.

'Four?' She crinkled her nose. 'I thought you said that you had two brothers?'

'I do.'

She knew then she had definitely said the wrong thing, and immediately apologised. 'I'm sorry…'

'You weren't to know.' He didn't elaborate

straight away, and neither did Felicity push, but after the longest pause it was Karim who broke the silence. 'I am the third son. Ahmed was the second. Zaraq is seventy percent desert. Ahmed was into desert racing. He was practising. His vehicle broke down and help did not get there in time.'

'I'm sorry.' She said it again and he held her gaze, even opened his mouth for a second to speak, then changed his mind.

Don't be. He'd been about to repeat her very words. *He caused this mess.*

There was no bill to summon—just separate rooms to go to.

It was the part of the night she always dreaded.

They walked slowly to the lifts, where a few people were waiting, and Felicity's heart was hammering in her chest as he stood and faced her.

'Thank you,' she attempted, 'for a wonderful night.'

Karim was about to say that it didn't have to

end there, but he hesitated. She was jangling with nerves, so he decided to soothe her with his mouth; he would play with her hair, his skilled lips moving in… He would let this lift go, Karim decided as the doors pinged open. His lips would meet hers and then he'd take her to his room in the next one!

His mouth was moving in. She was his sweet dessert to linger over—he had waited twelve hours, and he was more than ready to be rewarded for his good behaviour now.

For Felicity, there was just a sliver of in-decision. She felt the weight of his lips, the bliss of his mouth on hers, then relaxed and gave in. They were alone at the lifts now, his hands loosely on her hips as his mouth worked on. Fear was replaced by pleasure, and a tiny curl was unfurling in her stomach. An empty lift opened, and she pulled back her head and stared into his eyes—because if he asked to see her again, even though she lived miles from London, even though it would be difficult, maybe she would say yes...

His mouth was on hers again, pulling her closer in, and it felt sublime to kiss him back without thinking. It was tender, but with intent, his tongue sliding between her lips, the thick scent of arousal suddenly closing in as if suffocating her. She jerked away again, because even if it wasn't tonight with Karim it would be soon. The inevitable day would come where she'd have to tell him she was frigid. She simply couldn't face it.

She saw the whip of confusion in his eyes as she fled to the lift and he called her name.

'Just leave me,' she sobbed, tears blurring her vision as she tried to make out the floor numbers. She ended up pressing more than half the buttons, so that the lift stopped and started almost at every floor. She wasn't scared that he'd chase her, just mortified by her own fear, choking down sobs as she swiped her card and stumbled into her room.

It was hopeless!

Soon her stunning grey dress lay in a puddle on the floor. Sheathed in lacy underwear, she lay under the sheets, curled into a shameful ball. She was ashamed of her own behaviour, knew she'd made a fool of herself and embarrassed him—he'd been kissing her goodnight, that was all.

It scared her how much she'd enjoyed it.

But she'd been stupid to try, Felicity was fast realising. Stupid to try and pretend that she was normal.

And very foolish to pretend with a man like Karim.

CHAPTER FOUR

STEPPING out onto the freezing grey street and heading for the underground, Felicity just wanted to get home.

Her clothes, as promised, had been laundered and delivered, and looked better than when she had put them on this time yesterday morning. She had set her alarm for six, determined to get out early and not to have to suffer the embarrassment of seeing him at breakfast.

She'd overreacted appallingly—she knew that.

A simple goodnight would have sufficed.

But it wasn't his kiss that had terrified her, it was the thought of where it might lead— where, with a man like Karim, it *would* lead.

She couldn't stand the shame of a disappointing end. Better to just walk away now. Karim oozed sexuality—and she could hardly beat him down with a stick, hardly keep chatting her way through dinner only to dodge his caress at the end of the night.

'Morning!' She hadn't noticed him jogging towards her, and she jumped when she did. He was dressed in grey sweats—a world away from the suited man she had dined with last night, but still impossibly gorgeous. Slightly breathless, he gave her a guarded smile. 'Off to get your train?'

'The line's running, apparently—I just rang and checked.'

Karim couldn't be bothered with small talk. He was annoyed, and glad that he'd caught her so that he could tell her so.

'You really didn't have to run off crying last night—saying no works very well for me.'

'I just…' She screwed her eyes closed in confusion and embarrassment—because she *had* kissed him back, for a moment had actually forgotten. He deserved some sort of an explanation—except it was impossible to come up with one. 'I just felt things were moving along too fast.'

'It was a kiss,' Karim said. 'And good kisses tend to move things along.'

He was still annoyed—but not just with her.

She was a *nice* girl. And nice girls wanted romance, kisses, flowers, phone calls—none of which Karim minded. But he wanted sex too. He stared down at her miserable face and it moved him—because if he'd had time on his side she might very well have been worth the effort.

Only he didn't have time.

'I've got to get going,' Felicity said, and he had to get going as well—back to his last taste of freedom before he took on the full weight of the crown.

So why was he calling her back? 'What if I want to take you for dinner tonight?'

'You'd have an extremely long drive!' Felicity attempted a smile, but it wavered when he shrugged.

'I don't mind travelling,' Karim said.

'Let's just leave it.' Tears stung her eyes as she stared at this beautiful man, who deserved so much better than her truckload of issues. 'Look, it isn't you, it's me!'

The pedestrian crossing was bleeping, the little green man waving her over—she could see the underground and just wanted to dive into it, wanted to fade into oblivion in the crowd. She shook him off and ran—but she was wearing heels and he was wearing running shoes. The crowd swallowed her, and she hoped she had disappeared into a mass of dark suits as she took the escalator.

Karim was enraged—confused and enraged! Who *was* this woman who used his lines? Who *was* this woman who denied his kisses, his invitations? Did she know who he was? He plunged into the underground. Okay, she didn't know just *who* he was, but that was part of the game—he won on charm alone.

Except with Felicity he wasn't winning.

'What's that supposed to mean?' He was beside her, with people tutting as he stood where they wanted to walk. He pressed in beside her, taking the escalator with her.

'Just leave it!' Felicity hissed.

'I don't want to.'

'And you always get what you want, do you?' Felicity's voice was curt—derisive, even—as she looked at him and saw him for the rich, spoilt playboy that he was. 'Well, not this time.'

They were off the escalator now, and he took her wrist. 'What are you running from?'

'You!' she said loudly. 'You just assume that I'll sleep with you because you bought me dinner—'

'I just offered to drive for hours to take you to dinner again…' Okay, he'd had no intention of driving—his pilot would have taken care of that side of things—but he had offered her way more than he intended and yet still she refused him. 'What's so scary about that?'

'Nothing,' Felicity snapped. 'Can't you accept that I'm just not attracted to you?'

It was a lie, an utter lie, and he dashed it with his mouth, kissing away her fibs. She could hear the tube train screeching into the station, feel the rush of wind around her legs, the thick flow of people walking past. But they all faded as he pressed hard into her. His tongue parted her lips and she felt flames lick around her stomach, felt a stroking deep inside that she'd never felt before, that none of Paul's fruitless attempts had ever yielded. And still Karim kissed her, his mouth capturing hers so thoroughly she couldn't breathe, didn't want to breathe, could only think about kissing him back.

'I beg to differ.' He pulled his head back.

She broke down then, in a way she never had before.

Karim stood for the longest time, then

pulled out an immaculate handkerchief and flinched just a touch as she blew her nose on his royal coat of arms. He should walk away—because it wasn't his problem, and clearly there *was* a problem. He was here for his final fling, his last taste of life before he took on full royal responsibility.

But he felt responsible *now*.

Tears rarely moved Karim. Hers did.

Walk away, a voice told him. He could not.

After a brief hesitation he took her in his arms, curiously relieved that she didn't stiffen or shrug him off. Unfamiliar tenderness—compassion, even—was filling him as he led her away from the underground and further complicated his life.

CHAPTER FIVE

'SHE didn't suffer…' Karim said to Felicity, but for the benefit of the curious onlookers as they took the lift to his suite. 'We have to take solace in that.'

Her face was in his chest. Her tears were at the gulping stage now, and from the depths emerged the glimmer of a smile. It warmed her that he would do that for her—would soothe the sting of shame as her private misery was momentarily on public display.

She could only vaguely remember getting back to the hotel, with him holding her, leading her through the streets. She had baulked at his offer of a secluded table in the restaurant, and she might live to regret the folly of her ways, but at some very deep level she trusted him. After last night she knew that for Karim no meant no, and the fact he was a doctor helped too. But it wasn't just that. Yesterday something had been triggered inside her, and Karim was the source—the source of a feeling that had always eluded her. And though she'd tried to walk away, now she willingly walked back.

Even in her highly emotive state there was a slight flash of wonder as they stepped into his suite—if hers was gorgeous, this was truly a palace—yet all she felt was safe. There was actually nothing sexy in it. She sat on his sofa and centred herself for a few moments as Karim rang down and ordered breakfast, then poured her a large brandy. She shook her head.

'It's seven a.m.!'

'We don't choose when these things happen!' Karim said, and so she took a sip, and then another. She shivered as violently as she had yesterday, after the accident, despite the warmth of the room, but it was she who broke the gentle silence.

'I shouldn't have accepted your invitation for dinner.'

'Are you involved with someone?' Karim asked, because that would make sense. Their attraction had been so fierce it would have been hard to deny it—easier, perhaps, to lie a little, to give in to the forces that had propelled them from the moment he had walked into the conference room.

'We broke up.' Felicity took another sip of her drink, then put it down—because nothing could calm her till she admitted the truth. 'I'm not very good at relationships.'

'Neither am…' Karim started, but then halted. Because even gentle humour was out of place at this time.

'There's no point starting something. It's not fair to you and it's not fair to me…' She wasn't making much sense. 'Paul and I were

together for a year and we weren't able to…
I mean, *I* wasn't able to…'

She actually couldn't say it, but Karim got
to the painful point. 'You were unable to have
sex?'

'Yes.'

'You know I am a doctor?' He watched as his
words were absorbed and she nodded. She
understood that at this moment he *was* a
doctor—which was maybe why she felt safe,
maybe why she had let him lead her to his
suite. He was a doctor—*another* one who
would tell her it could be sorted. 'And I am
telling you—you are not frigid.'

She shook her head. She had heard it so
many times before.

'Felicity.' His voice was firm and so
assured—so absolutely assured that she
wanted to believe him. 'You are *not* frigid.'

Yet no matter how she might want to believe
him, how assured he sounded, she knew better.

'I've seen doctors, psychologists. I had a

boyfriend for a year and we tried everything. All I ever feel is scared.'

'Did they work out why?' He didn't flinch as she spat out a mirthless laugh. 'Your sister is ill?'

'She's anorexic,' Felicity said. 'Well, she's recovering.'

'And your mother suffers with extreme anxiety?'

'I know all that.' Felicity clawed at her scalp—because she was sick of it—sick of going over and over it in the hope of a different outcome. Always the result was the same. 'My father was a controlling drunk. There was no abuse as such…' She hated all the questions, the assumptions—because they were all wrong.

'Abuse does not have to be sexual or physical to be abuse.'

'No…' Felicity breathed, glad that at least he understood that—that her father's controlling ways had been enough to damage her in a way that wasn't as obvious as her mother's or Georgie's. She had been left with an intense private fear of giving trust, of losing control, that couldn't be logically explained.

He didn't make her try.

'You have never once felt aroused?'

'No. Never.'

'Not once in your life?'

'No…' Her eyes darted to his, and then back down. This was the reason she was here—because yesterday she *had*! Yesterday Karim had flicked a switch. She didn't know how, but she wanted to know why.

He stood torn with rare indecision. He was moved by this beautiful selfless woman who delivered babies, who had so bravely saved a life yesterday, who put her family first and was, for whatever reason, holding a part of herself back, too nervous to trust. The clock was ticking on his last days of freedom. He could be out there enjoying himself, but he actually wanted to be here. He wanted to spend his last days with this shy, deep stranger, to bring passion and joy into her life—and of course there would be a reward for him too!

'I'm not being a doctor now,' he said. 'Because as a doctor I cannot speak like this. But as a man I can fix it.'

'Paul said the same,' Felicity sneered—because his was a typical response, such an arrogant thing to say, and it told her he didn't really understand.

'I'm not Paul, though.'

She pressed her fingers into her eyelids, because he had made a vital point.

'And I am telling you that you are *not* frigid. I assure you, this can be fixed.'

'How do you know?' She was angry at his assumption. 'How do you *know* that I'm not just going to feel worse if the world's sexiest—?' She stopped then, watched his beautiful mouth curve into a smile, and she cringed back on the sofa but sort of smiled too.

'Compliment accepted,' Karim said—and

then he stopped smiling, serious now, and knowledgeable too. 'I can fix it. Because to be frigid, or whatever you choose to call it, means you are unable or unwilling. You think you are unable, but you *are* willing. In the lecture theatre, when we stood in the dark near each other, were you aroused then?'

'I don't know—I don't know...' She was trying to stand up, like an animal trying to escape, mortified, confused. He held her wrists.

'Suppose we took it slowly...' Karim watched her through narrowed eyes. 'Suppose you said yes to dinner tonight.'

Tears were spilling out of her eyes as he deliberately said the wrong things, and he knew he was right then—knew he was right to say what he said next.

'So why don't we get *it* out of the way—and then...' He forced her chin up to see his smile. 'You can actually enjoy dinner.'

'I don't know...' she breathed. 'I don' t even know how I felt yesterday.'

'You *were* aroused,' he said. 'I could feel it, I could smell it, and I could taste it.'

'How?'

'Because I was aroused too.'

So she hadn't been imagining it.

And as he watched his words settle in her mind, Karim knew he was right to do what he did next.

'This,' Karim said, guiding her hand to his thigh, 'was how you were feeling.'

She could feel him beneath her hands, long and thick and hard, and so huge it really brought her no comfort. She went to pull her hand away—because if she hadn't been able to accommodate Paul, then how the hell could she accommodate Karim—but he was speaking on, talking in low, sensual tones that held her hand there. 'As I stood in that room I could feel it, and I could feel *you.* I wanted to go over to you...' She could feel him stretch beneath her fingers, feel a stirring in him just as she had felt herself. She felt him harden as he spoke, yet still her hand stayed. 'I could of course do nothing about it. I stood there like this and saved it for later.'

'For later?'

He glanced to the left, to the bedroom and the massive rumpled unmade bed. 'Last night after dinner I could have called many women. Yet I wanted *you*.'

She could feel his manhood steeling upwards, feel the strength of his erection beneath her fingers. A sick excitement built in her as she pictured him on that very bed. She was not even looking at him now, just holding him and staring at the bed.

'I *had* you last night, Felicity.'

Oh, she could feel a terror building deep within—only it didn't exactly feel like fear, more a nervous flurry that was usually evident in her chest, but was much lower now, as his voice rumbled on, as he grew in her hand.

'I stroked myself and thought of you, and I know you did the same.'

'No.' She jerked her hand away. 'I didn't. I *can't*,' she begged.

'But do you *want* to?'

Did she?

It was a dangerous situation, and yet somehow she had never felt safer. He was beautiful, and for the first time she was starting to feel it was not impossible.

'Yes…' It was the most honest she had ever been—because right here, right now, she *did* want to. With him, with this man who knew how to hold her, how to kiss her, how to talk with her. This man who had known to take her by the hand and walk her back to the hotel. It was reckless and dangerous, and there wasn't a hope of justifying it, but if she couldn't do it with him today then she could never do it with anyone.

Here, with this beautiful man, was her chance to start her life over, to cast aside the demons that plagued her. She had never been so attracted to anyone. Oh, yes, physically—

but *everything* about him enthralled her. His rich voice, his piercing eyes. And as for his smile… A smile that was turned on her now…

'What if I can't?' Felicity asked—not angrily this time, but because it was what was worrying her the most.

Still Karim smiled. 'You worry too much.'

Someone knocked at the door and Karim stood. Felicity's eyes glanced down to his groin, to all that she had felt, but there was no real evidence of it now—just a long shadow against his lean thigh. As Karim called the butler in, it was like a bubble bursting, and real life invaded. Terror caught up with her as she realised what she had agreed to.

'I am going now for a shower.' He gestured to the table that was being laden with food fit for a king. 'You will eat.'

As the butler exited discreetly, Felicity stood, unsure what to do.

'Eat!' Karim called from the shower, as if he could read her mind.

Eat?

She didn't want to eat, she just wanted to get it over with—which was undoubtedly the wrong way to think, but it was how she felt. She was tempted to turn tail and run, listening to the running water. Oh, Karim didn't know the extent of her *problem*, couldn't understand just how real her fear was. That despite honest, desperate efforts by Paul she was so closed up he couldn't enter.

Karim took his time showering. He wondered, as he dried off and pulled on a bathrobe, if she would still be there when he came out.

Last night he had wanted her, yet he had sensed her nerves, and as his guest it would have been wrong...

He had wanted her, though.

She had him curious.

Karim shaved himself, and thought about her, then grinned in the mirror as he recalled her words and nearly cut himself as he stared at 'the world's sexiest man'!

She was cute, Karim decided, paying closer attention to his heavy overnight growth but his mind was still on Felicity.

Karim read women well—he'd had plenty of practice. Yet Felicity was a challenge—which suited Karim fine.

He loved two things in life—women and challenge. Felicity was both.

He knew she was terrified, knew she was probably expecting him to lie her on the bed and devour her for hours, yet he also knew that would be pointless. She wouldn't relax when in the back of her mind she would be waiting. Despite her protests, despite her insistence that she didn't like it, he *knew* he had aroused her back there in the lecture room. And Karim mused on *that* as he walked out of the bathroom, to see her nervously sitting there, as if she were waiting for a dental extraction. He realised that only when it was impossible to do anything did she relax.

'I have to make some phone calls,' Karim

said. 'Important calls. I am sorry, I cannot avoid them.'

'Of course!' Felicity smiled, but inwardly her heart sank.

As he leafed through his diary—no doubt wondering where he could pencil in their 'sex hour'—he chatted away in Arabic on the phone, and then switched to English. 'Tell him to call me back in five minutes!' His voice was dark and full of foreboding. 'If he calls back one minute later the deal is off!'

He turned to her. 'Why don't you have a bath and relax while I make these calls?' Karim offered.

Though he probably thought he was saying the right thing, Felicity was tempted to pick up her bag and run. If only it were so easy, she thought wryly. How many bubble baths had Paul run for her? There was no chance of her relaxing, knowing what was coming...why couldn't anyone understand?

'Look—' she gave a brittle smile '—I really think I ought to just go…'

'One moment.' His phone was bleeping again, and he took the call. But with his free hand he pulled her towards him, rolled his eyes at the intrusion, and chatted as he idly stroked her face. Then, still in between talking, he kissed her cheek—lots of tiny little kisses as he spoke on. When the call had ended, he kissed her more thoroughly.

'Have a nice bath, and then I will be free…'

'Okay…' He was so nice to kiss. Clean-shaven now, he smelt of soap and cologne. His hair had been damp against her cheek as he'd kissed her neck, then returned to her face.

'Stay there,' he growled as his blasted phone rang again. He put it on speaker phone, rested it on the dressing table behind them, and proceeded to kiss her again as a nasal voice droned on in the background. 'They will be calling me back in a few moments.' Karim smiled at her as he barked his instructions to the phone. 'Bath!' he ordered—only she didn't want to go.

She could feel his arousal pressing into her, could feel his tongue mingling with hers, and it was like being back in the tube station. There was a delicious pull low in her groin as he pressed himself into her.

'Were you really?' Felicity pulled away. 'Last night—were you really thinking of me?'

'Oh, yes…' Karim said, lifting her onto the dressing table. He parted her knees slightly, pulling her skirt up around her hips, and Felicity felt her stomach tighten. 'When you lie in the bath, think of me as last night I thought of you. Like this…'

Fascinated, terrified, she stared down as he parted his robe, her throat constricting at the sight of him. Fear and hopelessness gripped her because she could *never* accommodate him. And yet he was so exquisitely beautiful. His hand stroked his magnificent member, his fingers loosely gripping the dark skin that she wanted to touch too.

'I thought of you in that dark conference room. I imagined forgetting everyone was there and walking over...' He was slowly nudging her knees apart with his hips, stroking against the silk of her knickers. She badly wanted to touch him. 'I thought of lifting your skirt...' He could see her arousal on her panties, and he touched it with his tip. He took her hand and guided it to him. She bit on her lip as she felt his velvet-soft skin and the power beneath it.

'Later,' Karim said, 'when I am not so busy, when I have taken this call and you are nice and warm from your bath...'

He was fiddling with her panties, pulling them down in one lithe movement, taking them over her ankles. Then he returned to stand before her, stroking her intimately with the tip of his erection. 'When there is no chance of us being disturbed...' He undid her blouse, shrugged it down to her shoulders, then unhooked her bra so her breasts were loose. Lowering his head, he suckled slowly on one nipple, dragging it out as still he pressed at the top of her legs. Her body twitched with each feather-light stroke. Then his mouth returned to hers, kissing her deeply, his tongue probing her, darting in and out as she unfurled inside.

Karim was always prepared, always aware of the value of his seed. Condoms were dotted everywhere in his life, and easily he opened a drawer as still he kissed her. 'Here.' He handed her a condom.

'We can't *now*…'

'Of course not. We will take our time—we have all morning—but it is good to practise.' He unwrapped the tiny parcel. 'Later, after your bath, you will slide it on like this…' Her hands were shaking so much she almost dropped the slippery thing. 'When you know how to do it, it will be much easier. I will show you…' He placed it on his tip and then took her trembling hands. 'Now, roll it down...'

She was terrified she'd scratch him, but she did as told, watching it unfurl over his gorgeous length. 'See,' Karim said. 'It is easy.'

Karim was glad it was on as he parted her and ran his erection over her sweet place; he knew that precious warning drop had already escaped. He *had* imagined her last night—but she was so much sweeter in the flesh. So pretty and pink and wet, and she was a virgin. Well, suffice to say he was ready! He stared down at her tentative hands and hoped he was doing right by her—because her beauty deserved it. He could hear involuntary moans escape her lips as his thumb worked her clitoris and his fingers crept to her entrance. He felt her tighten, felt her tense refusal, and knew rather than hoped then that he was right to do it this way.

She felt his fingers *there* and she panicked. But as they moved away she relaxed a touch.

His blasted phone was ringing again, and

she knew he had to get it—except she didn't want him to, was kissing him hard as he pulled back.

'I have to get that!'

'I know.'

But he was still kissing her as the phone clicked off, kissing her harder and harder as the message bank bleeped.

'He'll call back…' Karim groaned his apology. 'Bath, Felicity.' He was right at her entrance, smiling a rueful smile. 'You deserve my full attention, and when you come out…'

He was right there, right *there*, just nudging a little, with tiny, tiny thrusts that went nowhere and yet shot her to orbit, giving her a glimpse of what maybe could be done. Then the blasted phone rang—their five minutes were clearly up.

'I will just take it… You go and…'

'Okay…'

'I really must take it.'

'I know.'

He was staring down at his sheathed erection, just there at her entrance. Felicity did the same.

'Soon I will have the whole day.'

'I know.'

The phone was silent again. He was a tiny way inside her, just the tip of him nudging her, and she was still staring down. His phone would start trilling again soon, and she knew when it did that he'd have to answer. But she didn't want him to.

'Look!' Karim gently ordered her, and she did, staring down at where he was, watching as he pulled out a little way and then pressed in a little more. He shrugged off his bathrobe, his whole delicious naked body in front of her, and she could feel her thighs shaking, feel a pit of want as he slid in just a little more. It was starting to hurt, and she knew she would spasm, but she was saved by the phone. There was utter regret in his eyes as she looked up.

'Now, if you will forgive me, I really have

to…' And he did. Holding her eyes, he thrust deliciously in, watched the shock of fear as he stabbed inside her, watched the surprise, the bemusement and then the wonder. If it had been anyone but her he would have come at that second, it was almost killing him *not* to come, and yet he wanted her to relish this moment. There was no triumph, just tenderness as he saw the rapt expression on her face as she looked down.

Oh, it had hurt—did hurt—yet it was a delicious hurt. For Felicity it was like a bizarre out-of-body experience. She was watching it, feeling it, yet unable to comprehend that it was happening to *her*. He absolutely filled her, guiding her hands to feel him, to feel him slide in and out, till she could look no more— because she was weak, leaning on his shoulder and sucking it—biting it, maybe— as her legs wrapped around his back. And then she felt it.

The *it* she'd never felt was emerging, the

tremble in her thighs spreading, a flash of heat darting up her spine as he bucked fiercely within. And it wasn't gentle, it was *fabulous* as he pulled her off the dressing table, and finally she came. Karim pressed her right into him, holding her, supporting her, as her body gave what she thought it never could—the delicious stabs of her first orgasm. She wanted to scream, but she held back. And then he was groaning and thrusting. And, yes, she could scream now—but instead she sobbed, a deep, sweet sob as he climaxed inside her.

Karim was dizzy.

He came often. But not like this—never once like this. He felt depleted—his thighs ached, the small of his back ached. It was as if he had dragged on hidden reserves to deliver all of his best. He couldn't even take her to his bed for a moment, just stood as he lowered her down.

'Thank you…' she gasped, as weak and as dizzy as him. She stood till the world caught up, and then let him take her to his bed. She sat on the edge as he undressed her, garment by garment, kissing each newly exposed part of her body and then lying down on the bed beside her. He held her in the crook of his arm and felt her warm skin. 'I loved it…' Her voice was more normal now. 'I never, *ever*, even in my wildest dreams…'

Her hand slipped down. He was about to tell her no, that it was too soon, too tender—but nature never ceased to amaze him. Her pleasure was so transparent, her wonder so catching, and he watched as he rose to greet her. And for Felicity—for her—he knew that he could do it all over again.

CHAPTER SIX

FOR three years, at some level, Karim had known this day would come.

Late afternoon his phone had buzzed quietly—not his regular phone, which he had long since turned off, but the one phone that he never could.

He had taken the call in the lounge, listened to the news and sat with his head in his hands in silence for a full five minutes afterwards. Then he had walked back into the bedroom, his gaze falling to where she slept, and all he'd wanted to do was climb in beside her, rest next to her soft skin and disappear. He wanted to wake with her in his arms and smile in relief as he realised it was just a dream. But to sleep now would have been to waste what he knew was his last taste of freedom.

The last few minutes in his life of being Karim—because, despite being the third-born son, he was being groomed to be King.

This day that should never had come—had never, when Karim had been a child, been anticipated. The third of four boys, relatively safe from the prospect of succession, he had run free. His mother had loved him with more abandon, the press had been less interested in the dark, wilful young Prince than in his elder brothers.

His elder brothers, Hassan and Ahmed, had been groomed, of course—Hassan the successor, Ahmed just in case. But for Karim, and later Ibrahim, there had been more freedom. It was a freedom that their mother had fought and begged for, and had been won only for her younger sons. Three of the boys had inherited some of their mother's features. Hassan, the eldest, had her piercing blue eyes but none of her joy or lightness, Ahmed, the second boy, had a lighter complexion and hair and had in-herited her high-strung personality too.

And young Ibrahim was a true mix of both—royal and abrupt, like his father, yet dashing and wild, like his mother.

Karim, though, was truly his father's son.

He was, his father had said in a pensive moment, the one who would make the best King.

Decisive, arrogant, Karim held an innate strength, a deep streak of privacy that belied his public persona. Even when his mother's indiscretion had been exposed and she had fled, shamed, to England, Karim, the closest to her, had been the only brother who had refused to cry.

It was how it had to be.

There could be no pardon, no erring from the rules—she was the wife of the King.

To Karim it was simple.

And, as third in line, it *was* simple: he could indulge his passion. While after their mandatory stint in the army his older brothers had studied politics and history, the young Karim had indulged his desire for medicine, heading to the UK, spending time with his mother, causing a stir on the social scene. A dashing Prince, he had had the young fillies of London eating out of his manicured hands.

At what point had it changed?

Staring out into the darkening London skies, Karim rested his forehead against the cool window and watched the cars, taxis and shoppers below enjoying the anonymity London afforded. He remembered the first time he had felt it, that shiver of realisation, a feeling he would later recognise as dread, sliding like black fingers around his heart. He felt it occasionally at first, then more regularly, until now each morning he awoke with a tight band around his heart.

Hassan had married. Karim remembered well the pride and the jubilation in Zaraq. Remembered too laughing at his father's concerns when it had been two years and no heir.

'There is plenty of time...'

Then it had been three years, then four, and then finally the news the country had waited for.

A baby due in April.

In February he had come—too soon for the little scrap of life named after the King. Karim had held his tiny nephew, Kaliq, on that last day. As a doctor he had known at first glance that no machines or technology could help. When neither Hassan nor his wife, Jamal, had been able to face it any longer he had held Kaliq in the palm of his hand, stared at the little life that was too weak, too frail, and yet so wanted, then held him to his cheek as his life had slipped away.

Those first voices of dread had started to speak up, but he had quashed them, dismissed them out of hand. Because if Hassan could not produce, then long in the future, if the King should die, there would be Ahmed.

Ahmed. Despite the grooming, despite the bravado, Karim had always known that his brother was fragile emotionally—just how fragile Karim had refused to consider. Burdened by the prospect that one day he might be King, Ahmed had one day taken his four-wheel drive into the hostile desert. Suicide was a sin, so it had been called 'heat exhaustion'.

By November the country had been plunged into mourning again.

Nothing was ever voiced.

Nothing had ever actually been voiced.

As third in line, Karim had always indulged in his passion for surgery, but as the line of succession had shortened, so too had his theatre and patient list. Slowly he'd been moved away from the hospital and from direct contact with patients. Instead he built a new hospital and a new university, trying to ignore the voices. Because if he acknowledged they were real…

Today they were real.

Today they spoke.

You are strong, Karim said to himself. You will be a good leader for the people.

He knew he was strong. And he wouldn't acknowledge, even to himself, the deep and buried truth.

Instead he pushed it aside and chose to get on with what he had been summoned to do.

The room was still and dark when Felicity awoke, stretching luxuriously. For that moment all she felt was peace—not a smudge of regret for what had taken place.

Karim was standing by the window, staring out on to the street below. Just as she was about to smile and greet him, she stilled. She saw the grave expression on his face, the weary set of his shoulders, and a chill of foreboding swept through her.

'Karim?'

He came over, forced a half-smile on his grim face, and sat on the bed beside her.

'You looked so peaceful that I didn't want to disturb you.'

'Is something wrong?' There was a different energy to him. They had made love on and off throughout the day, and Felicity had shared with him not just her body but her mind. She had told him how she adored her family, how it was tearing her apart to leave them even for this short while, how she adored her work, her friends. Bit by bit she had revealed herself to him, but now, as she stared up at his strained face, despite his tender words she realised Karim had revealed so very little.

'My father is ill.'

'I'm sorry.'

'He has been ill for some time, but I have just found out that he has been admitted to hospital. I have to leave tonight for Zaraq.' His face was stamped with pain.

Felicity knew he was telling the truth, and she moved to comfort him as he had her, but even as she held him, he was unreachable.

There was tension in his shoulders, and when he pulled back his voice sounded formal rather than tender.

'I don't know when I will be back.'

'Will you call me?' Oh, of course one should never sound needy, but she *was* needy—needy of him.

'I did not expect to have to return so soon. Felicity…' He wasn't finding this easy—wasn't finding any of it easy. He stared at her. She looked confused and gorgeous, and he wanted to take her with him, but he couldn't. She didn't even know who he was—and more than that he couldn't inflict it all on her. She wanted romance, flowers, phone calls, Karim reminded himself. She wanted her family and her friends and the freedom in her body that he had just given her. He couldn't, wouldn't do it to her. 'It will be busy when I get home. Things are very different for me there.'

'So that's it, then?' Hurt, angry eyes met his, yet there was a dignity to her as she dressed, a proud dignity as she pulled on her clothes. And there was something else about her too—since this morning she had grown up. Before him now stood a proud, strong woman, and Karim knew that this day had played a large part in that.

Felicity knew it too. Oh, she was hurt, and bitterly disappointed, yet somehow she also felt strong. Of course he must go to his father. Of course they could never be…

But something beautiful had been taken away too soon, and it was with that sentiment that, instead of storming out, she walked over to him. And Karim held her. He held her in his arms as if he never wanted to let go.

'I will have a car take you home.'

'Karim, I live miles away…'

'You are not getting a train.' His phone was ringing again, and this time he answered it, talking for a second or two before clicking off. 'My plane is being prepared.'

'*Your* plane?'

He checked himself, determined not to confuse her further. 'I am sorry. Sometimes my English is confusing. I have to be there soon. I have booked my ticket. I have to leave in half an hour.'

He didn't want to go. She knew that. She could feel it in the hard kisses that he showered on her, in the desperate lovemaking that ensued, could even feel it as he took her down to Reception and saw her to a waiting car.

The journey home was long, but Felicity wanted it to be. She needed to get her head around all that happened in the last twenty-four hours.

She didn't even know his surname—yet this man had changed her.

To anyone else it would sound cheap and sordid—a day of no-strings sex, with someone she would never see again—yet Felicity felt no need to justify to herself what had taken place.

Especially as, after she had taken the lift to her apartment and rummaged for her keys, when she paused in the middle of the corridor and saw a most exquisite bouquet at her door.

They must have cost a fortune, soft pink blooms of orchids, and with tears in her eyes Felicity read the note.

Never forget.
Karim x

How could she ever forget? Felicity thought, letting herself into the flat, staring at the blinking red light on the message machine and listening as Noor offered her a position in Zaraq.

The money was more than she'd been expecting; the only blight was that she had to leave within a week. Felicity knew it couldn't have been Karim's doing as, from the time of recording, the message had been left immediately after the information session.

Her mother's message urged her to ring the second she was home. Instead she crossed her modest flat and stared out of the window into the cold night sky. She imagined Karim up there, flying back to his sick father, and wondered if they might meet again. Because even if his life was complicated, for Felicity it was actually rather simple. She read the card one more time.

Never forget.

Oh, she'd never forget—because every second of their encounter was etched indelibly on her mind. And anyway, Felicity realised, letting the tears spill now, she'd never forget because already she loved him.

CHAPTER SEVEN

THERE was no time to dwell!

Not a single thing she could do about it!

In the week she'd had left she'd had to fill in paperwork, decline her prior job offer, and attend endless friends and family farewells—as well as reassure her mother and sister that she wasn't disappearing for ever.

And even though she knew she'd be back it was so hard leaving.

Standing in the airport, Felicity hugged her fragile sister close.

'Look after the flat,' Felicity said, trying to pretend she wasn't worried about how Georgie would cope living alone.

'Of course I'll look after it! I'll be fine—stop worrying.'

'I'm not worried,' Felicity lied. She wished for the same lucky star that had sent her Karim to shine on her sister, wished Georgie's problems were as easy to solve and she prayed that Georgie would be okay, that this essential separation wasn't going to set her back. 'You stay strong,' Felicity said.

'I will.'

'You'll ring as soon as you get there?' her mother fretted.

'I will,' Felicity assured her. 'But, Mum, I won't be ringing often—and you can't ring me on my mobile. We can't afford it.'

'I know,' she breathed. 'We'll be okay, darling.' Felicity's heart twisted with pride as her mother did her level best to be strong and brave. 'And so will you.'

Felicity hugged her mother and then she walked away, through the security checks and barriers with all the other tense passengers.

And as she entered to the boarding lounge, despite her doubts and worries, there was excitement too.

This was *her* time. This was *her* adventure.

For Felicity it wasn't about making money and saving for a deposit on a home, it was about clearing debts, about cleaning up the past and moving onto the future. And also, though she tried to curb it, there was a sliver of hope too as she boarded her flight— because, despite his firm words, there was surely a chance she might see Karim again.

It was a long journey but a comfortable one, even in economy class. Zaraq Air looked after its passengers.

Just, Felicity thought, as Karim had looked after *her* that magical night and day.

Putting on her headphones, Felicity flicked on her little screen, smiling at the tourist information film about Zaraq. She gazed at the images of sandy beaches, deserts and mosques, excitement building. Soon she would really be there…

It was talking about the royal family now. She listened as the narrator explained about the ancient kingdom, with a royal blood line so pure that its founders had passed on their proud name—each King a true Zaraq. It was riveting. Felicity watched the screen as soldiers marched smartly outside the palace, with the King of Zaraq waving to his subjects from the balcony, his family beside him.

And then Felicity's heart stopped.

Because there, smiling from the seat-back in front of her, dressed in full military uniform and looking stunning, was—as the commentator informed her through her headphones—Sheikh Prince Karim of the Kingdom of Zaraq.

It was as if her bowels had turned to ice.

Karim was a *prince*.

No wonder he had warned her they could never be together. It wasn't just miles that separated them, but a heritage that went back thousands of years.

'Your seat belt?' Felicity blinked as the stewardess reminded her, snapped on her belt, and sat in stunned silence as the plane began its descent.

Her first glimpse of Zaraq was through disbelieving eyes. She watched the blue Mediterranean ocean give way to yellow sands. The plane circled in a wide flight path, as if to mock her, letting her glimpse all the power behind the man and the vast abyss that separated them.

Golden sands as far as the eye could see one minute, and then, as the plane dipped to the left, she glimpsed Zaraqua, its ancient buildings huddled together. The cabin lights dimmed, and it seemed wrong somehow to be encased in metal, seeing medieval mosques, colourful markets, from such a modern invention. And then for a second she glimpsed it—the most spectacular building of them all, rising as if from the dust with the ocean as backdrop. What must surely be the palace.

That was Karim's home.

As the tyres hit the tarmac, as the brakes screamed and Felicity was pinned to her seat, it was nothing to the impact she was feeling as she landed in Karim's world.

As she entered the Kingdom of Zaraq.

CHAPTER EIGHT

'LEILA?' Her back was to him, and Karim watched his ex-mistress jump as he walked into his bedchamber. 'What are you doing?'

'Waiting for you.' She turned and smiled.

'You were not invited.'

'So?' She pouted. 'That never worried you before. I heard about the King, and I wanted to be here for you, to give you some comfort during these worrying times.' She ran a hand over his chest and Karim grabbed it.

'Leave.'

'Karim…' Her other hand moved to his crotch but Karim blocked it. 'Leave, Leila. I should not have to say it twice.'

'One last time,' she pleaded. 'Make love

to me one last time—we were so good together, Karim.'

And they *had* been good together—at least Karim had thought so at the time. Yet since Felicity there had been no one, no desire, no need for another woman. And it confused him, because there *was* desire and need but it was aimed solely at her.

At Felicity.

'Leave.' Three times Leila made him say it, and Karim's voice was black. Her tears didn't move him; her sobs only enraged him further. Karim summoned his guards to remove this woman from his life.

He would find another, of that there was no doubt, but the next one had—according to his father—to be his bride.

The thought made him shudder. His brilliant mind was bored easily, and the thought of waking to the same woman every morning chilled him to the marrow. He could take a mistress—he would probably *have* to—

Karim conceded. And his mind, as it always seemed to these days, flicked to Felicity.

He was tempted to ring her, to check with Noor if she had accepted the job at the hospital. But, no, it was too dangerous a time right now. Maybe when these next months were over, maybe when there was a suitable bride-to-be in the palace, when things were more stable, he would allow himself that indulgence.

Maybe, Karim thought, lying back on the bed as Leila's sobs faded in the distance, he could *keep* Felicity in London.

Pleased with himself, liking his idea, for the first time in a hellish day Karim smiled.

Felicity soon found out the meaning of hitting the ground running. She was met at the airport, as promised, by a fellow English nurse. Relief flooded her as she saw her name on a card being held up by a dark-haired smiling woman who introduced herself as Helen.

'Thank you so much for this…' Shy, awkward, and still stunned at discovering who Karim really was, Felicity had great difficulty listening to all Helen was saying.

'Don't worry; you'll be greeting people yourself in a few months. It's a great system. After orientation you'll be buddied up with me for your first few shifts.'

'How long have you been here?'

'Nearly a year,' Helen said. 'I'm going home for a visit in a few weeks, and then I'm coming back for another year. I only intended to stay for one, but I love the place.'

There was so much to take in.

Her accommodation was fabulous. She had a small apartment on the same floor as Helen's, and there was a gym and two pools— one for women, one for men. It was *bliss*, Helen told Felicity as she showed her around the complex, to dip into the pool after a hard day on the ward.

'You work hard while you're at work, but there's loads of leisure time too,' Helen explained. 'It really is wonderful once you get used to it.'

And for those first few days it really *was* just that—wonderful. Helen introduced Felicity to loads of ex-pats—friends waiting to be made—and gradually, as Helen took her to some other haunts, as she discovered the colourful, loud bazaars and blinked at the contrast to the designer boutiques in town, Felicity came to believe this was the best decision she had ever made. So busy was she by day she didn't have time to stop and think about Karim. She almost forgot she was here in his country, that he was nearby. It was only late at night that her mind wandered.

A shiver of excitement and fear filled her as she lay in bed. Here, in Karim's world, the palace was her view from the bedroom window. She ached for him, and some nights actually got up, pulled by strange longing, to stare out of her window and imagined him sleeping.

Or not.

Resting her head on the cold window didn't cool her as she thought of him lying on a bed not so far away. Maybe lying there thinking about her…

Her orientation days had been informative, but Felicity knew the only way she would really fit in was when she actually started working. She was grateful when Helen knocked on her door early for her first real shift, and walked with her through the hospital grounds and into the hospital. It was immaculate, like the most luxurious private hospital, except this was accessible to all.

'Except the royal wing,' Helen explained. 'If you think this is fabulous, you want to go and have a peek up there. It has its own nursing staff. It's used for royalty and diplomats and the like. The King's a patient there right now.' She nudged Felicity's attention to the tented city beyond the hospital walls. 'They're keeping vigil for him—he's very ill, apparently.'

'What about his sons?' She couldn't stop herself from asking, but Helen didn't turn a hair, just kept on walking. 'Do you ever see them?'

'Prince Hassan has been visiting daily, while the King is a patient, and there's always a bit of a stir when he arrives…'

'Isn't one of them a doctor?' Oh, so casually she said it—but Helen gave Felicity a small nudge as they walked. 'Hands off Karim! He's mine.' She grinned. 'Who told you about him?'

'I can't remember.' Felicity blushed as pink as her uniform. 'One of the girls said that one of the princes was a surgeon.'

'He used to be,' Helen said, 'and he still does the occasional list. But he doesn't do much now, so he's rarely around. He's too busy being a royal, unfortunately.'

'Unfortunately?' Felicity checked, her throat tight.

'I miss my fix.' Helen nudged her again, not noticing that Felicity wasn't smiling. 'I miss

swooning in the corridor when he stalks past—
not that he'd acknowledge me, of course.'

'Because he's royal?'

'No!' Helen laughed. 'Because he's a
surgeon—they're treated like royalty the
world over. Karim fitted in here perfectly.
Now, did you bring all your documentation,
like I told you?'

It was to Felicity's intense relief that Helen
changed the subject then. It took her till the
middle of the morning to work out that for the
first time in her life she'd been *jealous*!

Her first shift was spent mostly getting
security tags and photocopying paperwork.
For safety Helen locked it all up in the ward
safe, and gave Felicity the duplicates. There
had been a couple of instances of credit card
theft on the compound, but security were on
to it, Helen assured her.

Her pale pink uniform was practical and
comfortable, and Felicity soon found out that
pregnant women were the same the world

over. Some were thrilled, others excited, some stunned and a few upset. By the end of her first week she had dealt with them all, and was that day working a shift in antenatal.

'Mainly this clinic deals with ex-pats from the UK or America,' Helen explained. 'Dr Habib speaks perfect English and has an excellent reputation, so we tend to do the clinic this way. It gives women from the same background a chance to meet mums in the same situation.'

Certainly, from the lively chatter in the waiting room, the theory was working well.

'For the first visit we check obs and weight, and do a routine urine and pregnancy test,' Helen went on as they worked through their busy morning.

Felicity ticked little boxes, checked dates, and tried to ignore the little voice inside that kept reminding her that her period was due.

Late, even…

Felicity glanced at the calendar, trying to

tell herself she was only a teeny bit late, and assuring herself that she was being completely paranoid. Still, by the time lunch came around it was nice to take a break away from the ward.

'I'm on the labour ward tomorrow,' Felicity said as she and Helen paid for their meals in the large canteen. Though *canteen* wasn't the word Felicity would use for it, because it was nothing like the one in her old hospital. The room was spacious and airy, the food was prepared by chefs instead of being delivered via vending machines, and was quite simply delicious. Already Felicity was getting to know a few people, and she smiled to a couple of familiar faces as she and Helen walked over to a table. 'And then I'm in Theatre the next day.'

'And after that you're on your own—I bet you can't wait.'

'I've loved being supernumerary, and I love that I haven't been thrown in at the deep end, but I really am looking forward to working on my own.'

'And delivering your first Zaraquian!' Helen grinned and drained her cup. 'Okay, back to it.'

A hefty nudge in the ribs as they walked out had Felicity looking up, and her face paled as she saw the subject of Helen's attention. Dressed in a suit, chatting and laughing with a colleague, he was focussed on his conversation and heading towards the surgeons' lounge. Corridors could feel like very long things at times—because Karim saw her. His eyes frowned, his voice halted mid-conversation—and then normal services were resumed. He swept towards her as if she wasn't there, completely disregarded her.

As, of course, any surgeon would a nurse they supposedly hadn't met.

'Didn't I tell you he was gorgeous?' Helen said when they had passed, but Felicity didn't answer. She had caught a waft of his cologne as he breezed past, and her cheeks burned.

Karim had very clearly set down the rules. Yes, corridors were very long things. Because, had he chosen to, had he cared even a little about her, there would have been plenty of time for a brief smile.

'I'm just going to the loo.' They were back at Maternity, and Felicity needed a moment to collect herself.

'Again?' Helen grinned.

Yes, again, Felicity thought. Because even though she didn't actually need to go, she did need to check.

Again.

And *again* there was nothing.

She was being ridiculous, she told herself for maybe the hundredth time.

They'd used protection. Karim had been so careful. Her period was one day late, for goodness' sake—hardly anything to worry about, given the move, given the flight. Yet she took out the little specimen jar from her pocket, because she just wanted her mind to be at rest. It was no wonder she felt slightly sick. The different food, jet lag… She was being ridiculous and soon she'd have proof. Wrapping the jar in toilet tissue, Felicity placed it back in her pocket.

She didn't want to take a test home with her—there were Security everywhere and what if they checked her pockets?—but neither did she have the confidence or knowledge to go to a local pharmacist. Would they ask questions? Could an unmarried woman even purchase a test? She truly didn't know.

But though her head was in many places, her mind was still on her patients.

'Blood pressure's fine…' Felicity smiled at the chatty woman beside her. Jessica Hammel was forty-two, had four sons in high school, and was about to welcome baby number five.

'It doesn't feel as if my blood pressure's fine!' Jessica rolled her eyes. 'I can't believe I'm going to be looking after a tiny baby again.'

She blinked at the enormity of it all.

'I had a tummy tuck two years ago. Fat waste of time that was!'

Felicity smiled and waited for Jessica to speak further if she wished.

'I'm okay with it. A bit stunned, I suppose. Everybody thinks I want a girl.'

'Have you found out?' Felicity asked, checking her patient's scan report.

'Nope!' Jessica said firmly. 'Because, as I've told everyone, all I want is for it to be healthy. Though…' she caught Felicity's eye '…after four boys a girl would be rather nice. I think I've earned a bit of pink!' Her voice was a little anxious now. 'Dr Habib said that if nothing happened by this visit, then I was to be admitted and induced.'

She looked over to Felicity, who was eyeing the CTG reading and almost willing it to change. But this baby looked very comfortable where it was for now. If Felicity had her say, it would stay put for a little while longer. Still, she didn't have a say, and, as she had told Karim, she wasn't here to change the world. She took her patient off the monitor and chatted away to her, trying, as she always seemed to be these days, not to let her mind wander to Karim.

Felicity took a pipette and did a routine pregnancy test on her next patient—one of the lecturers from the university who had been undergoing IVF. She happily ticked the little box on the chart as the pink cross came up and signed her initials, before throwing the card in the bin. She turned to go, then changed her mind and opened up the cupboard that held the pregnancy tests, worried about taking one. Where she'd used to work nurses did it all the time—it was for that reason the tests were generally locked up. But she was here in Zaraq and she simply had to know!

She pulled out the little jar, seeing her hands were shaking, and performed the simple test. She jumped guiltily when Helen breezed in, pulling out trays and looking for some batteries for the Doppler machine. Felicity joined her in the search, as she was still trying to get acquainted with where everything was kept.

'You're doing really well. The clinic is running smoothly.' Helen smiled. 'Tonight there are a few of us going out for dinner—you should come along…'

'I might ring home tonight,' Felicity said. 'But thanks for the invite.'

'There'll be plenty more.' Helen shrugged. 'We're a friendly lot, all in the same boat…or the same desert. Who's that for?' she asked casually as she found the batteries and walked out, glancing over her shoulder at the test card.

For Felicity there was the most appalling moment—because a negative test would cause confusion, given they were in the antenatal ward. But Helen didn't notice the silence, just glanced at the patient file and answered her own question.

'She's a nice lady, isn't she? Dr Habib will probably send her straight for an ultrasound, just to put her mind at rest.'

'Sorry?' Felicity croaked.

'IVF patients,' Helen answered patiently, as she had all Felicity's questions through the week. 'They can't believe they're pregnant till they see it for themselves on screen.'

Despite the cool air-conditioning Felicity felt as if she were standing in the heat outside, as if the sun was beating on the back of her head. She was drenched with nausea and fear, and tried to walk casually across to the bench to comprehend why Helen was talking as if the card indicated positive.

'Let me know if you change your mind about tonight,' Helen said, walking out of the room, utterly oblivious to the chaos she'd left behind. The heavy door softly closed behind her.

Picking up the card, Felicity stared at the pink cross, telling herself she must have mixed the specimens up. But that argument failed in a trice—she was meticulous at that type of thing. Jessica's specimen had been thrown away before she'd even retrieved her own.

The card was wrong. Felicity's heart lurched in hope. Maybe it was a faulty batch. And then her heart sank again—because that would mean every test she had performed this morning had been on a non-pregnant woman—which, given they were in an ante-natal ward...

Her mind just staggered from hope to hope, like a lost child running frantically in the super-market for his mother, tugging every familiar coat and then recoiling when it wasn't her.

She *couldn't* be pregnant!

She couldn't be trapped in this country with no ticket home and not enough money for one either.

She couldn't be having Karim's baby.

A baby!

There was no comfort in that thought, no sweet feeling of peace or surge of maternal protection—her only feeling was unadulter-ated fear.

Two weeks ago she'd never even met him.

Two weeks ago she'd been a virgin.

Now she was in a strange country, where they didn't tolerate pregnancy out of wedlock, and if that wasn't bad enough she was pregnant by one of the family who made the rules.

She stared down at the card and the unpalatable truth hit her.

Yes, she was pregnant.

Pregnant by Sheikh Prince Karim of Zaraq.

CHAPTER NINE

IT WAS the longest, loneliest night of her life.

She rang her mother, trying to sound upbeat and happy, trying not to think about telling her.

Or Georgie.

She'd have to ask a friend to loan her some money for a ticket home. Or work for a few weeks and then break her contract and fly back.

To what?

She was already in debt up to her eyeballs. Lying on her bed, Felicity was shell-shocked, completely overwhelmed by it all. She stared over at the palace and thought how it mocked her tiny flat.

Single motherhood versus his kingdom.

He was responsible for this too, Felicity breathed.

She wouldn't make a fuss—would disappear with her baby from his life if that was what he wanted—but he had every right to know, and he was in every position to help. Slowly, slowly she calmed down…

For about eighteen seconds.

Someone else, Felicity realised as she was given handover on her early shift the next morning, hadn't had a very good night either.

Jessica Hammel had been given gel to ripen her cervix the previous evening and had spent an uncomfortable night. She had just started to complain about her contractions and had vomited, but there were no regular strong contractions to speak of, and Dr Habib was on his way to see her.

'Just keep an eye,' Martha the charge nurse said.

It was obviously nice for Jessica to see

Felicity's familiar face when she walked in to greet her and her husband, Garth.

'How are you doing?' Felicity asked, but Jessica didn't answer. She closed her eyes and clutched her stomach as a wave of pain hit.

'They're coming more regularly now,' Garth said to Felicity, rubbing his wife's back, as he had done on four occasions before.

Instinctively Felicity's hand moved to the patient's stomach, to feel the strength of the contraction.

'She doesn't look well,' Garth said, and privately Felicity agreed with him. Helen was standing by the bed, assessing her new midwife, and Garth was concerned for his wife and trying to tell himself he was imagining things. 'Mind you, it's been a while…'

Felicity nodded, worried that there was no tightening. She looked over to the CTG to confirm her findings. Jessica wasn't having a contraction, although clearly she was in pain.

'Helen?' She gave that wide-eyed smile that

was familiar to nurses the world over, which meant help was required, and then smiled back to her patient, who was opening her eyes now that the pain had passed, two hands on her stomach now, both Felicity and Helen, assessing the odd situation.

'I'm paging Dr Habib now...' Helen said—not that Jessica noticed. She was vomiting again, and her blood pressure was low as Felicity checked it. Far from being supernumerary now, she laid Jessica down and applied oxygen. She tried to comfort Garth too as she inserted an IV, and Helen urgently typed in the message to be sent directly to the doctor's pager.

'What's going on?' Garth was taking deep breaths, trying to stay calm, and all Felicity could do at this stage was answer him honestly. 'I'm not sure, but Dr Habib is on his way.'

'Is it the baby?'

Felicity's eyes flicked to the foetal monitor, to the strong, regular heartbeat, and swallowing a fraction she shook her head. 'The baby seems fine. Dr Habib will be here soon.'

In moments in fact, and Dr Habib was instantly concerned. He examined his patient and it was clear his excellent reputation was well earned. He didn't dither. Instead he told Helen to summon the on-call surgeon, and Felicity's heart tightened several times as she heard the word *Karim*.

He must have rolled out of the on-call bed instead of his undoubtedly more luxurious one at the palace, because he was there in a matter of moments, dressed in navy theatre scrubs. Instantly he commanded the room. And yet in an unexpected but very kind touch he nodded to Garth and very briefly shook his hand, explaining who he was, before he palpated Jessica's abdomen.

'I'm Karim Zaraq—the surgical consultant on call.'

Whether Garth knew of his title was irrelevant to him and irrelevant to Karim at this hour. Felicity watched as a very calm surgeon assessed a very ill patient and came to a rapid decision.

'Your wife has to go straight to Theatre. Till I get her there I cannot be sure, and there is no time to confirm my diagnosis with ultrasound, but I believe your wife has an intestinal obstruction. I need to operate—along with Dr Habib.

'Ring Theatre and alert them.' Karim nodded to Helen, who was already on it as Felicity prepared a trolley for the urgent run to Theatre. 'I need you to sign a consent form,' Karim said to Jessica's stunned husband, scribbling on paperwork as he spoke. Calm but concerned, he explained that though he had a provisional diagnosis until he operated he could not know exactly what was wrong—and that it was better in this case to act rather than wait and investigate. He held the man's eyes as he offered the pen, and added that he would do everything he could to save Garth's wife and his baby. Garth didn't hesitate.

Felicity and Helen both dashed with the patient to Theatre. Jessica bypassed Reception and was moved straight through to the operating room. Felicity and Helen pulled on shoe-covers and caps, and helped the porters and theatre staff to move the patient to the operating table as the rest of the theatre staff methodically and rapidly set up. The anaesthetist was lovely—Felicity caught a waft of an American accent as she chatted to her semi-conscious patient—and then it was all under control. Jessica was Theatre's patient now. An anaesthetic was about to be administered; her stomach was being prepped. Felicity and Helen were politely thanked, which meant they must leave, because—as the theatre charge nurse said—'We'll take it from here.'

Felicity wasn't looking for him, but her eyes found him. She saw him scrubbing up at the sink, washing each nail in detail. He glanced up and for a second held her eyes. With her eyes she wished him all the best for the operation, told him that she missed him, that she needed to talk to him, and his eyes told her the same.

And then he was back to his nails, back to doing what surgeons did—saving lives.

Jessica got the little girl she was hoping for. She was a gorgeous baby too, bonny and pink and covered in vernix. The baby was soon returned to the labour ward, where Garth met his daughter and spoke to Dr Habib, and then came the arduous task of waiting for news on his wife.

She *had* had an intestinal obstruction, Dr Habib explained, and considerable adhesions which had been caused by the tummy tuck. It would be a complicated procedure but, Dr Habib added, 'Her surgeon asked me to pass on that he is quietly confident that your wife will be fine.'

Felicity watched as Garth blew out his breath and she did the same. She was so grateful, as she popped in regularly on father and daughter, that Karim hadn't kept this man waiting. He had been aware of the agony of waiting and had offered some much needed hope.

It took a couple of hours for hope to be formally delivered.

Karim, tired but elated, smiled as he walked into the nursery, where Felicity was checking the baby's temperature as Garth watched anxiously on.

'Your wife is fine.' He got straight to the point. 'It was a difficult operation because there were a lot of adhesions. I had to remove some bowel, but I achieved a healthy anatomises—' He frowned and checked himself. 'A good union. There is no colostomy.' He carried on with the good news as Garth stood, tears streaming down his face, and then Karim moved onto the not so good—which, after all Jessica had been through, sounded like a walk in the park. 'She will stay in Recovery for a couple more hours and then she will be looked after on my surgical ward by my team. Of course she is postnatal, and has had a Caesarean section, but I would prefer that my team watch her. They know my ways, know the things I like to be called for…'

Helen was here now, telling Felicity to go on her break, and Karim didn't hang around—as Felicity moved off, so did he. Her respiration rate increased as she walked towards the staff-room, her heart pounding as she felt his eyes on her, heard footsteps behind her. She paused as he called her name.

'Felicity…'

She went to turn round, and it was at that point it all caught up with her: yesterday's shocking news, her sleepless night, the warmth of the theatre and Karim's black eyes waiting to meet hers. She was drenched in cold sweat, could feel it running between her breasts, breaking out on her forehead. Leaning against the wall, she was glad to see Helen over his shoulder, hear the question in her voice as she took in Felicity's grey face. But

Karim was already on it, seizing her arm before she fell, breaking her fall as the floor slammed up to meet her.

He somehow guided her to a side room with only the minimum of fuss. Not that Felicity cared by then. She was completely out of it. She came to at the horrible plastic smell of an oxygen mask, and saw Helen's kind, worried face as she let down a blood pressure cuff.

'Low!' She smiled at her colleague. 'My fault for not sending you for your break earlier.'

'I'm fine.' Felicity tried to sit up, but Helen pushed her down.

'It happens to all of us—the food, jet lag. Rest there...' She stopped talking then. Chatty, effusive Helen was suddenly silent. Karim had come back from wherever he had been.

'I have spoken with the nurse co-ordinator—you are to be moved to a side ward. Staff health—'

'I'm fine.' Embarrassed now, Felicity sat up, but Helen pushed her down, her eyes warning

Felicity to be quiet. 'It was a simple faint. I really don't need—'

'I have said what will happen,' Karim broke in. 'You are to be admitted.'

'I don't want to be admitted,' Felicity argued. Helen's eyes widened in horror, but she didn't care if she *was* arguing with a surgeon—or a prince, come to that. All Felicity cared about was *not* being admitted. Because there were many reasons for her to faint, but she knew the real one. 'I just want to…'

'Excuse us, please.'

She saw the dart of confusion in Helen's eyes at his request to be alone with Felicity, but Helen took her own advice and didn't argue. She slipped out of the area and they were alone. Felicity wanted him to scoop her into his arms, wanted him to hold her, to say that he had missed her, to say anything at all. All he did was stand there.

He gave nothing away—could not smile, could not hold her. Couldn't because if he did he would surely snap. He had operated throughout the night on what was meant to be his last 'on call'. The operation had been long and intense, yet he had loved it. He had stood under the lights and performed in *his* theatre as only a surgeon could. *His* choice of music playing, *his* team—the team that *he* had individually chosen. They had worked together for the very last time and then he had walked out to Recovery to speak with his patient—a halal butcher from the main street of Zaraqua, a man who had held his hand and thanked him not as a royal prince but as a doctor.

Unusually for a consultant, he had stayed at the hospital, had lain on the bed where he had slept as an intern, deciding he would hold onto his pager till nine—because he just couldn't stand to let it go.

At seven fifty-five he had been summoned.

He had run through the hospital with adrenaline chasing his heels, had walked into crisis and felt calm, had seen Felicity there, reassuring husband and patient. If there was one day in surgery he could capture this would be it…

This *was* it.

And now he had to walk away. He stared at her pale face on the pillow, knew he could drag her in deeper—or let her walk away.

He chose to give her no option.

'Tell me now why you do not want to be admitted.'

'I don't want any tests.' Her eyes were blinking rapidly.

'Because?' His mouth that had been wet was suddenly dry. He wished that she would answer, wished that she would prove his mind wrong.

'Because I'm pregnant.'

He heard the prison doors slide closed, heard the turn of the key not imprisoning him but *her*, his child. And he couldn't stand it. His mind flashed to Kaliq—to the frail babe he had held in his hand, the tiny babe who should have lived to be King. How proud Karim had been of his nephew as he had slipped from this life to the next.

No, he would *not* tolerate prison for his child, so he refused to even consider that it was his. She had to leave, had to go away—and *he* had to ensure that she did.

'Don't.' His voice was like ice. 'Don't even try it on me, Felicity. Don't even think of playing games with me.'

'It isn't a game…' Her voice was bewildered, reaching out to him, and he couldn't stand to see the pain on her features. 'Karim—I found out yesterday. I know we were careful…'

'Careful!' Karim breathed, angry now, in fact enraged—because she *had* to be lying, because this couldn't be true. 'I am more than *careful*! Do you know how precious my seed is? I don't go to the local chemist for protection. Do you think I would take risks with a whore like you?'

She couldn't believe the brutality of his words. The sexy, tender lover who had won her heart so easily was unrecognisable now. Each word spat a warning, each growled sentence told her not to even attempt to argue. 'Did you find out who I was, Felicity, at that introduction day? Use your little sob story, your ways, your wiles and pretend to be a virgin?' It was so much easier to loathe her than to love her, so much easier to send her away than to claim her now.

'I am...' she sobbed. 'I *was*.'

'Please!' Karim sneered. 'There was no evidence...' He shooed her away with his hand, dismissed her sobs, her story, as easily as he would swat a fly. 'There is no place for your sort here in Zaraq. I could have you arrested.'

This was a different man—a completely different man from the one who had held her. 'Karim, please. If you will just listen—'

'No. *You* listen.' He was standing directly over her, his menacing face silencing her. 'I will not let you smear my name with these lies. Because I know the consequences a woman in your position faces, you will be admitted tonight under my care. I will arrange for your contract to be broken. Your things will be packed and you will fly home tomorrow. A car will collect you. I will arrange your ticket.' He stared down at her and forced himself to say it. 'You will be generously remunerated for your services that day.'

'Karim!' she begged.

He was unmoved by her pleas. Whether or not she was telling the truth, in time she would realise he was actually doing her a favour. 'Enough—you do not argue with me. Tomorrow, Felicity, you leave Zaraq. If you choose to stay, then you deal with this dilemma alone.'

CHAPTER TEN

THIS wasn't the first woman who had lied to Karim.

And by the time he hit the changing rooms he had convinced himself she was a liar.

Because all women lied, Karim told himself as he showered and dressed.

His mother, who had kissed him goodbye as he left for school and said that she would see him that afternoon, had lied.

His father's lovers, who'd feigned interest in the young Prince only to discard him when his father summoned them.

And later his own lovers.

They swore he was their first, or that they

understood it was just sex—they too lied, because always they wanted more from him.

And now Felicity.

Sweet, virginal Felicity, the most precious of his memories, tainted now. She had no doubt been pregnant already and looking for a father. Who better than a royal prince?

Did she think he was a fool?

It was so much easier to be angry, so much easier to not believe.

All this whirred in his head as he marched through the hospital with his entourage. Khan, Karim's senior royal aide, had told him that the King had asked to see him.

He visited his father daily, but this time he had been summoned.

His father had asked that the nurses and the aides all leave, and seeing his gaunt, strained face, Karim fleetingly wished for the problems of a moment ago—how much easier *they* were to deal with than this was surely going to be.

'I have spoken with my surgeon.' The King's

once strong voice was now thin and reedy, and Karim stood, his back straight, his face an impassive mask, as the news was delivered. 'At this stage surgery is not an option.'

'Surgery is your *only* option.' Karim's voice *was* strong, his bedside manner steadfast and absolute—as it would be for any patient facing the appalling truth. A strong doctor, a strong man was needed to give bad news. The only indication that it was his father he was talking to was a flicker of muscle in his taut cheek. 'To live you need surgery. The tumour is getting bigger.'

'My heart is too weak. If they operate now I will die on the table.'

'I will arrange another opinion—' He stopped then. There had been so many opinions, and Karim trusted only his own. '*I* will operate.'

'Karim!' There was some strength still in the King, and he used it now. 'You are to stop this nonsense. You are a surgeon, but you are not a god. You cannot make miracles. I will not let you operate; I will not give you the guilt that will come when surgery fails. I am to rest, to be built up, given medication, and if my heart is strong enough *then* there will be surgery.'

'You might die waiting.'

'Karim, *this* you cannot control.'

'That is not your teaching—'

'It is the truth.' The King's response was direct. Two proud, strong men were facing the future and did not like what they saw. 'Karim, I am not scared of death. I am scared for my people, for my sons, for the turmoil I am leaving behind.'

'There is no turmoil,' Karim lied.

'Please—there is no time for lies or sugar-coating the truth. Hassan and Jamal—well, since Kaliq...' His voice faltered then, and both men remembered the tiny scrap of a baby who had lived only two days, the weak off-spring Hassan had produced, too fragile to carry the hope of the nation. 'There is still no sign of a baby—which means after Hassan there is no heir, no hope for the people. I know you do not want to be King, but that is why I have pulled you back from your work. You, my son, will have to step in. I have spoken with Hassan, and reluctantly he agrees that for the people of Zaraq there must a strong ruler, one who can produce heirs. Not him.'

'Then don't die yet.' Karim said, because to him it was simple. 'Just refuse to.'

'I will try not to,' the King said, 'but I will rest easier if I know that my affairs are in order, that the people have a future. You must marry, Karim. Your playboy ways end now—this very day. You will take a bride, you will produce children. Hassan will step aside. Even though he begs not to, he knows he must step aside…'

'What if Hassan *did* produce an heir?'

'We know that is not going to happen—again Jamal weeps this month. The people need to know that if their King dies the Zaraq line will go on.'

Karim was never swayed by emotion. He stared out of the tinted windows at the vigil that was being held, at the people who had no idea what the future might be without their strong King. An idea was forming in his mind, a germ of an idea that was growing even as he stood. It wasn't a new one either. A conversation like this had taken place years ago, but the strategy had been discounted. Karim resurrected it now.

'What if I told you there will be an heir?'

'I have said already—Jamal cannot—'

'There is a woman,' Karim broke in. He could not stand to picture her face as he said it, so he stared at his father—his King, his ruler. 'She says she is having my child.'

There was just a beat before his father answered. 'Then marry her, Karim, and Hassan will step aside.' To the King it was simple.

'What if it is not mine?' Karim challenged, hoping it would terminate the conversation, that somehow he could set her free. But the

King on his deathbed would settle for a lie if it meant that his people had hope.

Oh, it had been done before. The pure blood-line the people of Zaraq were so proud of was littered with hidden secrets. There had been affairs everywhere. Even his own brother Ahmed, so much fairer, so much paler than the rest…though doubts had never been uttered.

Karim could never raise a child that wasn't his own. But Hassan could—if it meant he would be King.

'You will do right by the people. I know that, Karim.'

Karim didn't answer straight away.

What if it *was* his?

Hassan would step aside, and Karim would be a better King, perhaps, with Felicity by his side. No woman had taken him to the heights she had, and he could have that again and again. There would be no need to stray. He could groom her to be a suitable wife, could teach her, make love to her… And as for their child… He leant against the window, because letting his mind go there brought him no peace at all. He couldn't even allow himself to think of that—couldn't allow feelings to enter into this at all.

He paced for a moment and then stilled, rested his gaze on the south-facing window, away from the people and the ocean to what mattered most…

The desert. It would not change in his lifetime.

Oh, the sands lifted and swept and moved in a blink—yet the constants remained.

He stared at the canyons that would remain for his lifetime.

He was a constant.

It was better that it *wasn't* his.

There would be a test soon, to confirm that fact. Felicity would see reason. What poor single mother wouldn't want a kingdom for her child?

Maybe his father would live, Karim thought for a wild moment. But without the peace

Karim must administer to him now it was surely impossible.

'You have to do the right thing for our people.' The King broke into his thoughts. 'I cannot rest till I know that the future of Zaraq is safe.'

Karim watched a small sandstorm settle— a regular event in the desert, blinding, paralysing, but temporary.

He stared at the canyons unchanged, at his grief that didn't matter in the scheme of things, and then he headed for a different window. Karim watched a wave pull back into the ocean, saw the swirl of a turning tide, and in that second his fate was sealed.

'Then rest,' Karim said simply. 'I will take care of everything. Rest and get strong, Father, knowing that whatever happens our people, our ways, are safe.'

CHAPTER ELEVEN

SHE'D told him.

Whatever his response, Felicity felt a certain relief that she had done the right thing—had given him the opportunity to be a part of his child's life and he'd declined it.

Maybe it was better this way, she thought, choking back tears as Helen came to see her early the next morning.

'Your things were packed last night...' There were tears in Helen's eyes as she spoke, but she was trying to smile. 'I grabbed a change of clothes for you. I figured you wouldn't want to sit on the flight in your nurse's uniform.' And then she was serious.

'You should have told me,' she said. 'I could have helped.'

'You know?' Felicity blinked.

'Well, most people don't faint and then leave rapidly in the first few weeks unless they have good reason. It is lucky that Karim dealt with you—he's spent enough time in London not to judge.'

Helen gave her a final cuddle, and it dawned on Felicity that it would never enter Helen's head there had been anything between herself and Karim.

'Here—I got these from the safe on the ward.' She handed over Felicity's paperwork. 'You wouldn't have got far without them.'

Another nurse wheeled her to the lavish hospital entrance, and to the limousine waiting to take her to the airport.

Her things had, as Helen said, all been packed for her. The driver told her they were in the rear of the limousine as she stepped out of the wheelchair the hospital had insisted on and climbed into the cool air-conditioned vehicle. She craned her neck for a last glimpse of the hospital, realising that in a few hours she would be gone from Zaraq.

But at least she would be on her way home.

Just another single mother-to-be, another father who didn't want to know. She hadn't been here for very long—no one would miss her.

Especially not Karim.

Zaraqua really was stunning, and Felicity watched it speed by for the last time through tear-filled eyes. Vast freeways sliced through the edge of the desert. How she would have loved her year here, Felicity thought, wondering about the sights she would now never see. She stared at the deep blue sky, the harsh landscape. This was her child's home. She tried to imprint it on her mind, so that one day she could tell her child about its origins—because its father clearly wouldn't.

She hadn't remembered the journey from the airport taking this long, and it was twenty minutes later that concern started to register.

The road signs were in Arabic, but there were pictures of planes to indicate the way. The driver seemed to have ignored them, turning off the main road and heading towards the glittering ocean.

Perhaps this was a quicker way? Felicity told herself. But, no, there was another sign for the airport indicating left. The driver was going straight ahead.

'The airport,' Felicity said, unsure if he could hear her through the glass partition. 'How far is it to the airport?'

On he drove. Felicity caught him looking at her in the rearview mirror, and suddenly she was nervous. She banged on the glass, demanding his attention, but still he drove on, and somehow, even before the white building loomed into view, even before they swept into a vast drive with the blue ocean glittering in the distance, Felicity knew where he was taking her.

Zaraq Palace.

She had seen it in the brochures, on the tourist film, from her bedroom window, but nothing could have prepared her for the imposing grandeur of it as they neared.

What did Karim want?

Her hand moved to her stomach. The tiny life inside her was the answer.

How foolish to think she could tell him and just leave.

How foolish to think it might be that easy.

As a midwife, Felicity chose to expect things to go smoothly, but she prided herself on being prepared for when things might not go well. It was important to smile and stay un-ruffled even when you were concerned.

She could see the driver's eyes on her in his rearview mirror, and knew he was waiting for her to react—she refused to.

She had nowhere to go—all her things had been packed and loaded and were in the car, and her documents were in her bag. Her passport was in there too, and apart from the life inside her it was the most precious thing she possessed right now. No one knew she had it. Everyone assumed that she only had the copies, not the originals, and instinct told her it must stay that way.

It was the one thing she clung to quietly as the gates slid open. The limousine glided past armed guards at checkpoints, and Felicity sat, her forehead beading with sweat, trying to wonder what Karim would have to say. Maybe he wanted to say goodbye, she told herself as the door opened and the driver came round to let her out.

A woman who introduced herself as Jamal greeted her, smiling warmly, but Felicity was unable to return it.

'Come.' Jamal led a shaking Felicity into the palace. The cool marble, the height of the ceilings—everything was daunting. 'We will have some refreshments…'

Tea was poured, mint tea that was refreshing, and Felicity didn't waste her breath asking about the purpose of the detour, knowing it would be in vain.

A man in a suit came then, and spoke for a minute in Arabic to Jamal who briefly translated.

'Karim will see you now—Khan will take you.'

She was guided through corridors with pictures of ancient ancestors hanging on the walls.

He rose from a low sofa as she entered a room, and he was wearing traditional black robes and a black and white chequered *kiffaya*. Tall, imposing and grim, he looked nothing like the man who had once held her—nothing like the man she had seen laughing and chatting—and Felicity knew she was meeting Sheikh Prince Karim Zaraq of Zaraq and it unnerved her.

His black eyes loathed her, as they had yesterday, and his brief smile was a fake one, of that Felicity was sure.

'Have a seat.'

He dismissed the man in a suit, then halted him. 'Would you like tea? I can ask Khan…'

'I've had tea,' Felicity said quickly. She just wanted to know was going on.

As Khan left, Karim turned and faced her.

'You say this is my baby?'

'It *is*,' Felicity said, glad of the chance to talk, to end things on more even terms. 'Look, I understand it's difficult and I don't expect—'

'Then we will marry,' Karim interrupted, and her eyes widened. 'Today, in an hour, we will be married.'

'We don't have to marry!' Felicity was flustered. It was the twenty-first century, for heaven's sake, they had been together for one night. He didn't have to do this. 'I just need help to get home. Maybe we can work out—'

'If this is my son, then you are pregnant with a royal prince. Of course we must marry.'

'No…' Felicity shook her head, ruing her own stupidity. She had frowned at Liam for not doing his research, for not knowing Zaraq's rules, and now she had in turn gone and done the same. She should have told Karim from England, Felicity realised, her panic growing. The palace was huge, but it seemed to shrink then, as she recognised the prison she had just walked into.

'If this is my child then there is no question that we marry—and the sooner the better. We will just have to hope that the baby comes a little late.' He flashed a very black smile. 'My guess, however, is that this baby is going to come early. Still, we will know where we stand in a few weeks.'

'A few weeks?'

'You will have an amnio, of course, and a DNA match will be performed.'

'No.' She stood up. 'Absolutely not.' She said it again. *'No.'*

But Karim just shrugged. 'Come—the papers have been drawn up. You will be prepared for marriage now. Hassan and his wife, Jamal, will be witnesses.'

'Karim, no!'

'Felicity!' He snapped the word—an impatient snap that silenced her. Then the room fell silent and he spoke again. 'You do not argue with me. I do not discuss things with you. But, given you are new to our ways, I will explain things to make you feel better. I will look after your family.' Karim stared coolly at her. 'There are merits to our ways, and looking after the extended family is one of them. Our marriage will bring peace to my father in his final days. In return, whatever the test results, I will secure your mother and sister's finances—yours too.'

'There won't be a test.' She wasn't going to take a test simply to satisfy his curiosity. 'This is your child, Karim.'

'Then,' he said patiently, 'there is no question that you can leave.'

It was like talking to a stranger. The beautiful, rational, sensitive man who had held her, to whom she had entrusted her body, must surely be there beneath the surface. But all Felicity could see was a strange clone of him.

'You come to this country, you live by our rules. We will marry today. When questions are asked, we will say this is a honeymoon baby. And if it is not mine...' Karim did not continue. Now was not the best time, perhaps, to tell her of his intentions for her bastard infant!

'Won't your people expect a big wedding? How are you going to explain?'

'My country is holding its breath for the King. It would be crass to hold a party now. For now we will be discreet, and in a few weeks we can arrange DNA testing.'

'No.' Her eyes shone with tears. On this she would not bend. 'No—it could be dangerous to the baby.'

'It is a routine procedure. We will then both know where we stand.'

'No.' She knew the more she resisted, the more Karim thought she was lying about him

being the father—but there was no way
Felicity would allow him to risk her child,
their child, just so that he might believe her.

'Felicity…' He was bored with explaining
now. 'You say that you are having my child—
you demand that I believe you—and then you
resist my proposal of marriage.' Karim truly
didn't understand. He accepted he had been
less than enamoured with the news she had
delivered, but now that he had proposed, now
that he was offering a *commoner* marriage, he
could not fathom her resistance.

He was right. Slowly it dawned on her—she
was having his child, was pregnant by a
prince. There wasn't much she could dispute.

All her clothes and her belongings had been
brought to a vast bedroom. Her life was contained in one suitcase and the handbag a maid
had placed in a large wardrobe. A scented
bath had been run, and in minutes she had
been relieved of her clothing. The handmaid-

ens now chatted excitedly as they prepared the bride for their Prince. They oiled her body, and her scalp too, and then tied her hair so it hung in a long coil over one shoulder. They rouged her lips and cheeks, and kholled her eyes, then dressed her in her wedding costume—a white beaded hand-embroidered gown that looked heavy but, when slipped over her head, Felicity found was actually light. Her head was wrapped in a veil, and her feet were placed in beaded slippers.

She was ready to meet her groom.

She stood and sat as instructed.

She knew that in this she had no say—but her mind was working overtime.

Karim was her baby's father.

Despite his harsh words yesterday, despite his cool demeanour today, somewhere within was the man she had fallen in love with. Somehow she knew she must reach him, and this was her only way.

It felt surreal as she walked into a large

study. Jamal was smiling, greeting her, and a man who must be Hassan nodded. Karim merely gave a nod of approval as she entered.

It did nothing to soothe her nerves.

'Karim…' Her eyes met his as she made a request she was quite sure he would refuse. 'Can I ring my family first?'

'Of course.' Again she had read him wrong. He even helped her dial, and she stood dressed in her finery, in a study looking out over the desert, her groom by her side, and heard her mother's anxious, excited voice at her daughter's unexpected call. Felicity closed her eyes and knew she couldn't tell her. Knew that until she had sorted things out with Karim she couldn't burden her family with all this.

In minutes she was married. The celebrations would take place later. She put her thumb print on a document and apparently she was his. And now, unless she wanted to jump out mid-flight, she had no choice but to sit as a helicopter whirred them deep into the desert towards the red setting sun and Karim's vast tented kingdom.

Her first true glimpse of the desert was at dusk. Stepping out of the helicopter, she felt the sting of sand around her cheeks, the whistle of wind in her ears and the heat of the day that had been absorbed by the land. Then she felt his hand on her elbow as he guided her across the sand to a huge tent. As they reached it, they stepped into a small entrance and Karim instructed her to remove her slippers.

'Here,' he said. 'Put these on.' Her feet were slipped into another pair of jewelled slippers, which seemed rather pointless, but as he parted the drapes and she padded through she understood why. There was no sand inside—the desert floor was smothered in thick patterned rugs, the walls of the tent too. Lanterns cast light and shadows as Karim parted swathes of silk and led her deeper within his desert abode.

Somewhat shaken and stunned, she stood quietly as he introduced her to his staff: a woman called Bedra and her husband, Aarif. They seemed delighted by their arrival, and guided them further into the bowels of the tent, where a lavish feast awaited them.

They were seated on cushions, apart and opposite each other, and a heavy purple runner was laid between them as Bedra served food and drinks on a low tray.

Felicity was poured some tea, and Karim instructed her to drink the syrupy brew that tasted of mint and sugar. Each mouthful, Karim explained to her, was part of a necessary ritual.

The food was endless, all eaten with the hands: Bedouin bread with olives and camels' milk cheese, pitta wrapped around richly spiced lamb. It was delicious, but she was too nervous to eat. Still she tried, because Karim was eating, and she was sure it would be rude to refuse. Yet the more she tried to eat the more Bedra served and the more Karim ate—until she was sure it would never end.

'Karim.' She gave a nervous swallow, not wanting to offend. 'All of this is delicious, but...' She couldn't speak of the baby in front of Bedra, but she truly couldn't eat another thing or she might offend him in a way that was unthinkable.

Karim, the haughty Prince who had rebutted her in the hospital, who had married her because he could, was now smiling. 'You are full?'

'Yes!' she hissed in a loud whisper. 'I can't eat another thing. I don't want to be rude...' She shook her head as he pushed his plate away and summoned Bedra to clear the tray. 'You carry on, though.'

'I'm not hungry either. But you see...' He was almost laughing, and that beautiful smile she had once been privy to dazzled her now again. 'I must not rush you. Custom says I should eat till my bride or my guest is full. Only when you are finished…'

She was almost smiling too—well, not almost, she *did* smile. 'You could have told me that before the camel milk cheese!'

And she glimpsed him again—glimpsed the Karim she had so quickly and heavily fallen in love with, the man who was the father of her child. And somehow, somewhere deep inside, Felicity knew this could work.

As Bedra approached, she took Felicity's reluctant hands. 'She is going now to paint you,' Karim explained. 'Henna for beauty and luck and health.'

Bedra painted Felicity's hands, and her feet as well as an intricate coil of flowers that crept up her calves and forearms. Yet all she wanted was to be alone with Karim.

'They are our witnesses,' Karim explained. 'Soon we will be alone.' Karim took her hand, slid on her finger a silver knotted ring that was studded with turquoise and agate and decorated with symbols. Karim's voice was serious. 'This symbolises not just two lives, but two families that are now intertwined.'

'Meaning?' Felicity asked. Perhaps not the most romantic response, but she wanted to know—wanted to know about his ways so that she might understand him better.

'It means that your celebrations I applaud and your problems I help with.' He stared into her eyes. 'Your family is mine. There is no burden that is not shared. This is what it means to be loved.'

She must be drunk on mint tea, because calm invaded her. This was her love that greeted her. This was the father of her child. And, yes, he was different here, yes, tradition invaded, but as she was taken aside—as Bedra smeared her body in fragrant oils and slipped a flimsy white muslin gown over her head and then directed her to his sleeping chamber— she was barely nervous. Because finally they could be alone.

He watched her walk over, her hennaed feet and hands stunning on her pale skin, her blue eyes dazzling, and the thin nightgown revealing her feminine shape.

Every night she would be his.

The rules had been waived now that she carried a child, and it meant that every night he could have her.

He must be gentle, Karim reminded himself as she padded towards him. His needs did not matter when the kingdom was at stake. He must remember that she was with child.

And then she was at his bedside. Shy and nervous, but decorated for him and forever his.

He pulled her down beside him. As he kissed her he could smell the oil in her hair, could feel the body that had aroused him so, and for once duty was a pleasure.

For Felicity, any nerves had vanished when he held her—just as they had the first time they'd made love. He slid off her nightgown and kissed each waiting breast in turn.

His lips moved up to her neck and then on, deliciously, to her waiting mouth. And finally he was kissing her—heavy, deep kisses that urged instant response. Her body leapt at the memory of him. Here in bed they could communicate. Here they could discover each other again and work out their differences.

As his fingers went to a place that was already moist, Felicity knew that this was the one thing they had in common. Her legs were parted by his knees and she let them relax. She was having his baby. He was her husband.

His hand reached over her head, and at first Felicity didn't know what he was doing. As he opened a small drawer in the heavy wooden bedhead and produced a sheath she was confused.

'It's a bit late for that,' she pointed out breathlessly.

'It is not just for—' He didn't get to finish. She slapped her hand hard across his cheek.

'How dare you?' She spat, then recoiled on the bed at his expression. Felicity wondered, in fact, how dared *she*. But she would not be so insulted.

'How do I know?' he demanded of her. 'Have you any idea the number of women who try this? Two weeks!' He shook his head at the improbability of it. 'I was using protection.'

'Then why marry me?' Felicity demanded—but Karim couldn't answer.

She was covering herself with her nightgown, her face wounded and angry, tears in her eyes. He wanted to believe her, yet he could not allow himself—because if it *was* his child she carried then unbeknownst to her everything had already changed, would change again.

He had to believe the baby was going to be Hassan's. Had to detach from the baby she grew inside. Because one day so must she.

He climbed out of bed, and when she saw he was holding a dagger, running his finger along the blade, there was a terror in her soul that she had never before experienced. Here in the desert, here amongst his people, who would respond to her scream? She watched. The blade was so sharp as he ran it along his finger that blood trickled, and then he looked over, saw her fear, and his face was as cold as granite as it registered.

'You imagination runs too wild. You are not a prisoner. I would never force you,' he sneered. And just as quickly as that he lay down the dagger, walked over to the bed and smeared the silk sheet with a trickle of his blood. 'I cover for your lies.'

'Why won't you accept that this baby is yours?'

'When I get the test results, then I will believe it.'

'There will be no test.'

'You do not argue with me.'

'Oh, but I do, Karim,' Felicity said. 'You *chose* to marry me today. You *chose* me to be your wife, and now you have me. I will respect your ways and your traditions in public, but here in private I will always speak—this is me. There will be no threat to my baby's safety just to satisfy you, and there will be no condoms just because you cannot trust that you have been the only one. So,' Felicity concluded in a voice that was shaky but somehow assured, 'it looks like there will be no consummation.'

'You do not leave here till our marriage is consummated.'

'Then we'll die in the desert,' Felicity replied.

Karim just shrugged. 'I have told you how it will be,' Karim said, and then he climbed into bed and turned his back to her. 'When you're ready, you will come to me.'

CHAPTER TWELVE

MAYBE they *would* die in the desert.

As the days moved slowly on, it became clear that neither of them had any intention of changing their mind.

Absolutely *she* would not give in—would not sleep with a man who offended her.

And absolutely neither would Karim.

He took her out sometimes. This land that looked so barren and bare was, Karim explained, full of gifts if only you knew where to look.

He was right.

In the seemingly bare desert he showed her landmarks, canyons that moved maybe ten inches in a lifetime, and the simple, endless rule of a sun that rose and set and always offered direction.

There were oases too—a full day's walk from each other. He took her once in his four-wheel drive, and they picnicked by one.

'They prove the land is fertile,' Karim said, stretching out on his back and staring up to the sky. 'You just have to know how to treat it.'

There was a response there on her tongue, but to her credit she chose not to offer it. She was biding her time till the Karim she loved returned again.

Bedra was her only real outlet. They chatted as Bedra dressed Felicity, or did her hair. But Bedra was always covered in a black *abaya*. How Felicity wished she would take it off, so she could see her face when she spoke to her. One day she asked Bedra about it.

'I do not wear it at home. There I can be myself,' Bedra explained. 'But here, at work…'

This upset Felicity—not a lot, but it niggled. For all their chatting, for Bedra it was work, and Felicity didn't want it to be like that. Bedra's husband, Aarif, tended to Karim, and sometimes when she was resting in the afternoon, while Karim wandered in the desert, she heard Bedra and Aarif laughing. She wanted it to be the same for her and Karim—because Aarif treated Bedra as if she were golden.

She asked Karim when he returned that day from the desert.

In a black robe and unshaven, he didn't look very approachable, but still Felicity asked—although she didn't much like the answer.

'Of course he is nice to her,' Karim said. 'Why would he not be? She is a good woman, a nice lady.' He frowned down at her. 'Why would he *not* be nice to her?'

'Well, you're not exactly nice and communicative with *me*.'

'Till our marriage is consummated you're not my wife.' Karim shrugged. 'Anytime you're ready, Felicity, you can find out how *nice* to my wife I can actually be.'

As the days ticked on occasionally they spoke, and sometimes even laughed, but both remained immutable on that point. And the more they spoke, the more he taught her of his people's ways and he learned of hers, the more impossible it seemed to be.

'Poor Hassan.' She was lying on the cushions eating figs, which Felicity had found out she liked—not just liked, *loved*. Pregnancy cravings, along with morning sickness, were starting, and figs—sweet, juicy figs—were the only food she could keep down. There was a lot to stomach now, and her head reeled as Karim told her about his family and what was expected of them.

'Why poor Hassan?'

'To *have* to be King.'

'He is honoured that he will serve his people. There can be no higher honour,' Karim said sharply.

'Then poor Jamal.' She refused to be quiet, even though she knew she was angering him. 'I don't blame them for not wanting children.' She shuddered a touch. 'It would be horrendous.'

'How dare you?' Karim barked. 'How dare you say our ways are horrendous? Their baby would be born to be King.'

'Which to me—' Felicity smiled '—would be *horrendous*. I'm just glad—infinitely grateful, in fact...' she paused as she took another bite of her fig '...that when you concealed your identity—'

'I did *not*.'

'When you *forgot* to mention you were a royal prince, I'm just glad that your name didn't happen to be Hassan.' She shook her head at the horror of it all. 'I could think of nothing worse. At least you get your freedom, get to follow your career...' Felicity frowned at that very thought. 'Why don't you practise any more?'

'It is not for me.'

'But you did?' Felicity pushed.

'For a while.' Karim shrugged. 'Then I realised I could do better for my people by overseeing the commissioning of the new hospital and university.'

'Do you miss it?'

He didn't answer.

'I mean, you're a surgeon…'

'Enough.' Karim terminated the conversation.

'I was just—'

'Then don't.' Karim clipped. 'When your husband says enough, when a royal prince says enough, you do not argue.'

'Oh, but I do. As I have repeatedly said—I will respect your ways in public, but in my home, which this blessed tent is for now, *my* husband will give me trust and respect and conversation.' She gave him a brittle smile. 'We're getting nowhere, I'd say.'

She slept in his bed, for the sake of the staff, but she would never give herself to him. The barrier he insisted on wearing was a barrier to her heart. Sometimes there was a fleeting glimpse of the man she had fallen in love with. Sometimes she would awaken in his arms, feel him wrapped around her, and wonder how she had got there, wonder for a moment what had taken place—yet sure that nothing had.

Safe.

Lying there one night, feeling him breathe, feeling his skin next to hers, she wondered how it could be. How, despite his vile accusations, despite his refusal to trust, despite everything, in the middle of the desert, deep in the dark with Karim, for the first time in her life she felt treasured and safe.

Karim wondered too.

Eternally vigilant, he felt her awake beside him and he wondered as to her thoughts, as to what Felicity lay in the dark thinking about. He wondered whether she was missing her family, and he knew she must surely be confused and scared.

He pulled her in just a little closer. Warm, relaxed bodies were so much easier to move.

Could her baby be his?

His hand went to her stomach, to stroke the

little scrap of life that was there inside, but he stopped himself. He could not let himself give in to emotion, because if it was his child then its fate was the same as his—and if it wasn't…

Karim's eyes opened and he stared into the darkness. The back of her head was inches from his face. How he wanted to bury his head in her hair, to kiss that neck. He could feel her warm bottom against his stomach. The hand that was wrapped under her held her shoulder loosely, and he was hard now. His fingers wanted to stroke at her breasts…

What if the baby *was* his?

Karim didn't do sentiment.

He never had and had thought he never would.

Speaking with his father, he had allowed his calculating mind to come up with a rapid solution.

For the sake of their people he would carry the weight of the lie, as would Hassan, and the King would take it to his grave. Once Felicity's test was taken and the baby proven not Karim's, Jamal's belly would appear to grow and the people would cheer.

Felicity offered a solution.

And now he'd had to go and do something stupid—like care. Care about the effect it might have on her. Every day she made him laugh inside, chatting away to herself even as he refused to answer. Every morning was better for waking up with her. Of course there were differences. He had assumed he would iron them out of her, but now he didn't want to.

How did he tell her that the career she loved must now end? How could he tell her that she was not just a princess but might one day be Queen—that her every last freedom would be gone?

She stirred a little beside him, and there, lying in the darkness, he didn't care about the people of Zaraq for the first time in his life. He didn't care about the people, he cared about *her*. Neither did he care if this child was a boy or a girl, he just wanted it to be *his*—wanted Felicity to be his too.

He felt her breathing grow shallow and quicken. His hand moved on her waist, bypassing her stomach and moving down, down, to her sweet, warm place, feeling her thighs part a fraction.

Tonight he would love her, Karim decided, and tomorrow he would tell her. And if she couldn't do it, didn't want to do it, then; maybe they would work something out.

He was right there, at her entrance, his tip already moist, could feel her oiled and ready beneath his fingers. So easy would it be to slip in, to sink in, to share and to trust…

Not a word had been spoken, not a kiss had been shared, yet she had never felt closer to him. She knew he was awake beside her, had known when it started that this was no idle, sleeping erection. And she knew too that he was thinking of her, even loving her a little bit. She had felt his fingers ponder over her belly and then move down, felt him softly stroke her, felt his mind wander and then return to her.

Parting her legs, she could feel him now, feel the swell of him, the tip of his erection nudging at her clitoris and then moving a tiny way back. She rocked against him, willing him, wanting him, desperate for him.

'Make love to me, Karim…'

'Your Highness! Forgive the intrusion…' Aarif was sobbing.

Karim swore violently in Arabic.

He was cursing and furious. How *dared* a servant intrude? If his father were sick his aide would ring. Nothing, *nothing* should disturb him in his chamber.

'Please forgive me, Your Highness,' Aarif pleaded. 'But Bedra is dying, bleeding….'

CHAPTER THIRTEEN

In a trice he dressed and sped through the tent. Felicity took a few seconds longer, but almost as soon she raced into the servants' quarters.

Bedra lay collapsed, her huge brown eyes terrified. Karim deftly examined her belly, and it was only then that Felicity realised Bedra was pregnant. The *abaya* had concealed it. Karim was speaking in Arabic, then quickly translating for Felicity.

'She is about six months pregnant.' There was blood everywhere as Karim delivered his stark diagnosis. *'Abruptio placentae.'*

In a hospital Felicity would have known what to do. There Bedra and her baby would both have a chance. But here in the desert, with help miles away, it was clear from the extent of bleeding they would rapidly lose them both.

Felicity rolled the woman on to her side, to help with oxygen delivery to the baby, and Karim barked rapid orders to a tearful Aarif, who quickly ran off.

'Should we drive her?'

'There is not enough time to get her to the hospital.' In one deft movement Karim scooped up the woman, carried her through long white corridors of tent. Felicity followed, confused as to where they were going. The desert was dark and cool as they stepped outside, and she was even more confused—because Karim had said it was too late to transport Bedra anywhere and yet one of the large four-wheel drives was speeding towards them. It stopped. Aarif jumped down and opened up the rear, and Karim ran towards the vehicle with Bedra in his arms. As Karim lay Bedra down in the rear of the vehicle Aarif was already pulling at leads, while Felicity stood, her nightdress billowing in the wind, unsure as to what exactly was going on.

Karim snapped her out of it. 'Felicity— come on.' He was strapping on a tourniquet as Aarif opened large labelled boxes, pulled out drapes. Here, right here in the desert, a mini operating theatre was being created. 'We must operate *now*.'

He was a surgeon, yes—but to operate, to perform a Caesarean section here…

'I am a surgeon,' Karim said, his eyes locked with hers. 'I know what I am doing.'

Aarif, on a strange kind of auto-pilot, where he was detached from his wife and baby in the hope of saving them, was slapping at Bedra's arm, trying to find a vein. It was then that Felicity stepped in. How and why didn't matter for now. They were in the middle of the desert in a four-wheel drive that looked like a mini-ambulance—and Karim about to perform a Caesarean section!

Karim was drenching Bedra's belly in

iodine; Aarif was pulling up drugs. 'I cannot give them,' Aarif said, handing her the vials, and Felicity looked at them. A strong analgesic, and a relaxant that would cause temporary amnesia. It wasn't a general anaesthetic, but in such a strong dose it would compromise her airway.

'Give them,' Karim said, setting up his instruments. 'Aarif will watch her airway. Felicity, get ready to receive the baby.'

His authoritative tone was welcome now. On Karim's instruction she shot the drugs into Bedra, but she was acting on her own instincts now, opening up a large resuscitation box and selecting the smallest equipment. Aarif took the ambu bag and bagged his wife, delivering vital oxygen as if he had done it a hundred times before.

The surgery was urgent and basic. It had to be. It was a classic Caesarean, a vertical incision, performed for haste. In seconds Felicity was being handed a scrap of life, and Karim delivered the placenta that had been ripping away from the uterine wall. It was the only way to stop Bedra from haemorrhaging to death.

Felicity worked on. The baby was flaccid, but responding to her resuscitation. She tried not to think, just to *do*.

Still her heart went out to Aarif. He looked over a few times, his eyes blank. This quiet man was guarding his emotions because it wasn't safe to have them yet.

Karim was calling to Aarif to give him more drugs, then packing the abdomen to prepare Bedra for transfer. Just as Felicity was about to ask Karim how she should summon help she heard the sound of a chopper landing.

Here in the desert Karim had saved not one life but two, against impossible odds, and now help had arrived.

He was shouting rapid orders to a doctor Felicity recognised from the hospital. It was Dr Habib running from the chopper to the four-wheel drive, but thankfully he didn't glance at Felicity, just headed straight for the mother. A paediatrician came to take over the infant's care. Aarif must have seen the fear in her eyes, and Felicity wondered whether he understood or misinterpreted it as shame at being uncovered. But he threw her a drape and hastily Felicity put it over her head.

Just not in time.

She saw the absolute shock on Helen's face. There was a stunned, questioning second, where both women swallowed the response on their lips. Then Felicity gave Helen a quick, urgent shake of her head, to indicate that this must not be acknowledged, and they did what they had to—got on with the job of preparing the little babe for urgent transfer. He had pinked up and was crying, but his cry was weak. To Felicity he looked around twenty-six weeks' gestation, and the paediatrician agreed.

Karim only relaxed when Bedra was under full anaesthetic and blood was dripping into her veins. Resting back on his heels, he stared over at the incubator, stared at the little life he had saved, and remembered his nephew, Kaliq, whom his brother had refused to hold. He remembered too Jamal's wailing, his father's tears—the whole country had been in mourning for the tiny little baby that had died in his hands.

And then he stared over at Felicity, chatting with the paediatrician, her eyes watchful on the child, and he knew that it would kill her to give her child away.

He straightened his back, refusing to let sentiment in. Because… Well, she might have to.

Only when they had loaded the mother and infant into the rescue chopper, the blades whirring as it prepared for takeoff, did Felicity manage to utter a few vital words to Helen— her only link with the real world, the one woman who could understand her predicament.

'I'll make contact.'

CHAPTER FOURTEEN

IT SHOULD have brought them closer, what they had shared, what they had achieved. Karim had been about to make love to her before the interruption, of that Felicity was absolutely sure, but as for the first time in his life Karim prepared his own bath his silence spoke volumes. He stonewalled her questions, pretending to be asleep by the time she'd bathed and returned to his bed.

'Karim?' She spoke to tense broad shoulders. 'You did so well out there…'

Yes, pretending to be asleep. Because in response to her question he proceeded to snore. And for all his ruthless ways, there were some redeeming features—and one of them was that Karim didn't actually snore.

It was worse than being told to be silent.

She persisted in her own way. She refused a husband who was less than he could be, refused to live with his silence. So at various times, as the days dragged on and they were truly alone in the desert, she chatted happily, though mostly to herself.

'I've cut myself,' she said—and she had, lounging on cushions, reading a magazine. She had a tiny paper cut that really didn't need anything doing to it, but she mentioned it just the same. 'I wonder if there are any plasters…' He was reading a thick black book, and he didn't look up as she stood, just lay stretched out on cushions. 'I know!' Felicity said brightly. 'They'll be in the fully equipped mobile theatre which just happens to be close by. I might go out and look…'

There was a ghost of a smile on the edge of his mouth as she walked past him.

'No, don't bother getting up, Karim. I'll get them.'

He caught her ankle, smiled up at her, and it was brighter than the sun outside. Scorching, warming, and it dazzled.

'You talk too much.' Still he held her ankle.

'You talk too little.'

'Sit.' He let go of her ankle and patted the cushions beside him, but she just kept on walking. 'Felicity,' Karim said with a rather strained sigh, 'why don't you have a seat and we can talk for a while?'

It was a little like being back in the restaurant—formal and awkward at first. But they avoided hot topics, like sex and babies, and given there wasn't much else between them spoke about the one other thread they had in common—their work.

'I just always wanted to be one,' Felicity

answered when he asked. 'I think I was *born* wanting to be a midwife. I love pregnant women, and I just adore newborns.'

But that was about babies… At every turn they couldn't avoid their issues, couldn't talk about her hopes to work in a natural birthing centre when she returned to England, because somehow it was too much to acknowledge that that hope was now gone. And she couldn't talk about her family, about her father and the legacy his alcoholism had left, because that would mean she trusted Karim.

And she didn't.

Finally, after a few stalled attempts, they spoke about Karim—which didn't help either, because the more that was revealed the more she liked him.

And the more confused she became.

'So you practise medicine out here?'

'With Bedra's help.'

It was Stockholm syndrome, Felicity told

herself—where you fell in love with your captor. Only she'd loved him long before that, and every moment he intrigued her more.

'It is like a mobile hospital,' Karim explained. 'I cannot practise any more at the hospital. It is not appropriate.'

'But you trained as a surgeon.' Felicity blinked. 'You *worked* as a surgeon.'

'I cannot be accessible to the people.' He frowned at her, and she chose to stay silent—chose instead of arguing just to listen. After a long pause, Karim delivered perhaps his first honest admission. 'I do miss it at times.'

Felicity blinked at the revelation, at his first display of emotion, feelings—proof that this remote man was actually real.

'You do not choose to be a surgeon. I believe it chooses you. And yet my country, my role, for reasons you do not understand make it impossible to do both. But here in the desert…' He was silent for a moment, as if drawing on the vastness. Even the wind wailing outside hushed for a moment as he centred himself and drank from the endless cup of wisdom this hard land brought. 'I can fulfil both. I can be a royal and I can heal—Bedra is a doctor,' he explained. 'She trained overseas and has returned to Zaraq to help her people. That is why I chose her to be here. The palace staff think she and Aarif are really servants. The Bedouin people are proud and remote, they would not line up at a royal tent for help, so Bedra takes help to them. That is the vehicle you saw, and with GPS she can summon assistance from the hospital. Sometimes, for things Bedra cannot do—she is not a surgeon—I go out with her…'

'You run clinics?'

'My family do not know. You are not to say anything,' he warned. 'I am working on a project to send doctors into the desert as part of the hospital rotation. However, for now I am servicing that need quietly.'

He made it sound as if he were running a brothel instead of practising medicine. How could saving lives be a *secret*?

'Change has to be slow,' Karim said at her furrowed brow. 'But there is change. There is the university, the new hospital. Women will not have to go overseas to study. I can work as a surgeon, and of course save lives, or as a royal prince I can slowly implement programmes that will change lives.'

As King he could just *do* it. Karim swallowed on that uneasy thought.

As King he could make more progress than his father or Hassan ever would. He loved his country, the traditions, its ways. But at times, at certain points, it frustrated him—angered him, even. Progress was so slow, yet as King himself more good could be done.

But it couldn't be about what he wanted, and it had nothing to do with Felicity, so he stood up and ended the conversation there.

Felicity didn't understand. He made her head spin. At every turn it was a different

Karim—the man in England, the Prince in his palace, and this doctor in the desert. But she wanted *him*—all of him. She wanted the blurred image to focus, for the many facets of this man to join into one.

She wanted *him*.

'I have to leave tomorrow.' He offered no explanation other than that, but this time Felicity refused to stay quiet. He always did this, Felicity was beginning to realise. Gave a little of himself and then regretted it, withdrew further and confused her more.

'Where are you going?'

'That is not your concern.'

'Karim, please…'

'My father has surgery in a couple of days.'

'And you didn't think to tell me? Karim, I am your *wife*.'

'A wife who refuses sex is a poor wife.'

'A husband who doesn't trust is a poor husband!' Felicity retorted, but he was prowling the tent now.

'When the helicopter comes to collect me, they will bring staff to take care of you.'

'No!' She hurled herself off the cushions towards him, scared of being left in the desert with strangers. 'No, Karim. I won't stay.'

'You will do as you are told.'

'No!' she begged. 'Surely your wife should be with you? Surely your family will expect that?'

His family expected *nothing* from her. He stared at her with black soulless eyes, held her wrists as she attempted to claw at him. Could she not understand that his family did not *care*, that all that was wanted from her was her baby—be it as Hassan's or his.

His.

For a second he relented, let go of her wrists and let her beat at his chest.

They did not care about her and *he* must not, Karim told himself, holding her arms again. But she kicked with her feet, beating her way into his closed heart.

'Let me come with you, Karim. Surely I should be—?'

Only his mouth could silence her, and it felt so good to feel her. He held her angry body in his arms and kissed her quiet. Every time she pulled back he kissed her harder. Now he could taste her, his tongue curling around her rigid one, pressing her right into him so that she could feel what she was missing, feel the heat that had been building for so long now. It was a heat he had refused to douse himself, relishing the challenge like a fast in the desert—because when she came to him, and she *would* come, how much sweeter victory would taste.

Her mouth was softer now, her body more pliant in his arms. But then she resisted again—and Karim dropped her.

'I have told you already—the desert is our home till the marriage is consummated. It is entirely up to you.'

CHAPTER FIFTEEN

SHE *had* to get back to Zaraqua. Would not be left in the desert alone.

Felicity lay in bed, pondering her baby's future. She wanted to give it the best chance to have a father, a loving father, and to grow up in a happy, loving home, yet it was up to Karim to take that chance—to trust in her.

How she hated him. Yet somehow she couldn't completely…

She closed her eyes as she recalled his lovemaking, the tenderness he could at times display, the insight that had freed her from her fear of sex only to plunge her into another prison.

He had to trust that this was his baby. On

that she refused to waver. Karim had to make love to her without protection or tomorrow she would be left alone.

As Karim prayed for his father and his country, Felicity drew her bath.

She had no seduction routine, no experience, but, drying herself off, she stared at the rows of glass bottles Bedra had prepared her with on her wedding night. She had poured rose water into the bath and Felicity did the same, then stepped into the fragrant water.

After, as she dried herself, she remembered Bedra's excited chatter as she had massaged Felicity's pulse-points with oil from tiny glass bottles. *Attar*, Bedra had explained—mixed fragrances. This oil was a heady mix of sweet amber, *oudh* and musk that would please the Prince.

'*Oudh?*' Felicity had asked.

'Wood,' Bedra had said. 'And I will place this dish of almond oil by the bed…'

'For perfume?' Felicity had asked, sniffing the bland dish, but Bedra had just laughed.

It seemed strange to Felicity to be massaging her pulse-points with oil of wood, but the fragrance was heady, and she remembered again him holding her that night, before it had all gone so wrong. She did what Bedra had done, and placed a slim silver dish of almond oil by the bed, waiting for him, as nervous as any bride on her wedding night.

He was 'too tired' to talk when he came to bed. He shrugged onto his side, with his back to her, and promptly feigned sleep. Yet she could feel his tension, could feel the black energy in the bed. When finally he did sleep he rolled over and held her, just as he did most nights. His hand in sleep on her belly made her weep.

She was protecting him from himself, Felicity knew. The man he really was would never jeopardise the safety of his baby. She turned over and stared at him.

She touched him.

She felt his body, reluctant, angry, even in sleep.

'I won't have the test, Karim.' She spoke to darkness, and didn't know whether or not he was listening, but she told him, warned him, begged to his soul to listen to her plea. 'I will not take the risk, however small, just to appease—'

'Felicity.' Annoyed with himself for having rolled towards her, he turned away from her again. 'Can we get through these next days?'

He willed sleep to come again. For Karim it was going to be a long night, made bearable only by having her beside him. He had considered taking a wife, but only for the sake of duty. There would be no real benefit to him. There had been so many lovers, so many women, and he had felt so many pleasures. Yet after the grim conversation he had had on the phone to his brothers insomnia had beckoned. He had never expected to feel peace this night—his father's operation looming, so many decisions to be made. Yet climbing in beside her, angry with her, with himself, with his brothers, with his father, suddenly all there was was the dark tent and silence, and the musky scent of her that gently spirited him to a better place. Hearing her breathe beside him had brought a rare peace that was unexpected.

Perhaps the future was a touch more bearable with her in his bed at night. And then she had awoken him.

And now he couldn't sleep.

He didn't want the test either—didn't want to find out the truth. This wretched time was only bearable because of her. Her scent was too heavy, too much woman lay untouched in the bed beside him. He considered asking her to go and bathe, to remove that fragrance so he might rest, except he didn't want to.

'I cannot sleep,' he admitted, half an hour of silence later.

'Would this help?'

'What?' He heard the nervousness in her voice.

'This.' Her hands were at his shoulders and softly she stroked them. She could feel the knot of tension in the muscles beneath the silken skin, felt him arch his neck as she smoothed a hard knot. 'Does it help?'

And because it seemed it did she gently guided him to turn to his stomach. She wanted this closeness as much as him— wanted this chance for Karim to see sense before morning came.

She knew what Bedra had meant now, was glad for the silver dish of almond oil that was by the bed. Felicity dipped her fingers in it, rubbed it the length of his back, moving her thumbs along his vertebra, her oiled fingers pushing into his loins then up towards his shoulders. She felt the tension seep slowly from him, and when it had, when he was relaxed beneath her, she peeled off her night-gown and turned him over. She dipped her fingers back in the oil as those black eyes caressed her body. She rubbed the sweet potion into him, slid it into the thick black hair, and cupped him tenderly in her hand.

'You know too much.' He grabbed her wrist. 'For one so innocent, you know way too much.'

'I know nothing,' Felicity corrected. 'Except what my body tells me—what your body shows me it wants.'

She meant it. Always sex had been feared, yet with Karim it was instinctive, her body, her hands, guided by more than her mind, by more than just thought.

The oil in her palm made him slide through her fingers, no grip in her hold as she touched him. Her two hands slid in perpetual motion, feeling him grow. Even as he slipped out of her grip the other hand was waiting to slide up to his peak, an endless tunnel that closed around his member. She was enchanted, feeling him grow strong in her hand, feeling his mind weaken. This proud, contained, distant man was coming close now to the man she had first met, the man she had first loved.

His eyes were soft as he took in her body. 'Your body is changing.' It was his first real acknowledgment of her pregnancy, and it made her melt.

'Feel it, then,' Felicity whispered, because touch brought closeness.

He oiled his palms with what she'd left on his body and slid his hands over hips that were rounder and softer now, then up to her breasts. Still her own hands worked on. He rubbed her breasts until she felt her thighs grow warm. His fingers stroked her tender nipples, slowly, slowly letting his hands take in the changes. He moved down to the soft curve of her stomach, his thumbs meeting in the middle, where their baby lay beneath. He stroked her pale flesh, and for Karim, for a dizzying second, there was a flash of a life that wasn't about duty or honour or country. It was about trust, doing things right by her. He could not stand the thought of a needle in her pale flesh, piercing into her uterus, disturbing their baby's slumber.

Their baby.

'There will be no test.' He said it, and then he said it again. 'There will be no test.'

She felt all woman, felt a shift between them. They could, here in his bed, be equals. It was something to build on.

'Felicity…' Her hands were like magic. A silver pearl of moisture was at his tip, and she rubbed it in till he thought he might weep. But Kings did not weep—nor Princes, nor men. With her, in that moment, maybe he could. 'I do not want to be King.'

She smiled down at him, held him with her eyes as still she stroked him.

'I would give *anything* not to be King.'

'You don't have to be….'

She didn't understand, and he was too far gone to explain, reeling from his own admission. From somewhere deep within she had reached in and pulled out the truth. Relief washed through him, allowing him to discard facts and believe she was right, that all he had to be was with her.

He did not want her hands around him now. He wanted *her*.

Her hips were slippery from the oil, but he lifted her, watched the glorious triangle of her thighs part over his erection. He massaged her clitoris, holding her there for a moment, because as soon as he entered her Karim knew he would come. He had never felt a woman around him without barrier, and as he lowered her onto him, felt the delicious grip of warm muscle, he thought he might die from the pleasure of a sensation he didn't want to end. He was stroking her inside and he could feel every twitch, every clench of intimate muscle, her delicious grip as he raised her hips and lowered her again and again. He refused to give in to his intense need, sliding her up and down his length and staring at her—at this woman who blurred everything, who made light of rules that were ingrained. How, *how* he wanted to trust.

She didn't need his hands to guide her now. Felicity was locked into a delicious rhythm. He was stroking her *there* now, but still looking at her, and she could feel the first waves of orgasm. She wanted him to come with her, her eyes pleading with him to join, to trust...

'I want to feel you come.'

Still he held back.

She was coming, so hard it made her scream. This was what he did to her. Took everything from her and yet held himself back. She was sobbing his name, begging him to believe that he was the only one, that this was *his* child to love.

He raised his hips and shot into her. He could do this every day, every night, for ever, if only he could believe.

He held her afterwards, his hands exploring her body as he wrestled with the demons of his mind.

His father had never forgiven his mother—had lived a lonely life since.

For what?

Karim had not slept well for two nights, he was aware of that. This crazy word *love* kept bobbing into his head, but he told himself it was lust as his hand crept between her sleeping thighs. Lust would have him hard again, lust would have him waking her from her necessary rest when now all he wanted to do was hold her.

CHAPTER SIXTEEN

IT WAS better with her here.

He had kept his word and brought her back from the desert—for how long he did not yet know. But as Karim visited his father it was easier knowing she was in the plush waiting area outside. Hassan was there too, and Jamal. Ibrahim was flying in and was due to arrive soon.

He didn't know in what way it was better, but as he stepped out of his father's suite his eyes went to hers first, blue jewels that shone from beneath the *abaya* she had chosen to wear, it was.

'How is he?'

'Weaker,' Karim said. 'They should have done this weeks ago, when I first said.'

'His heart would not have taken a long anaesthetic then.'

'Hassan and Jamal are going back to the palace once they have seen him,' Karim explained. 'I am going to meet with the surgeon and discuss his plans for the procedure.'

'I'd rather wait for you.'

'I may be some time.'

'Then I'll wait.'

After a moment's pause he nodded.

'Could I visit Bedra?'

He shook his head. 'It is too soon for the people to know. You might be recognised…' He stared into her eyes and relented. 'For a little while. Tell her I pray for her and her son too.'

The maternity ward was busy. Visitors were in each room, and nobody gave her a second glance as she strolled through the familiar ward—dressed in an *abaya* this time.

Aarif recognised her, though, bowing, overwhelmed that she would visit. Felicity quickly told him not to make a fuss, and then she saw Bedra, pale and tired on her pillow, but alive.

Her soft brown eyes filled with tears as they met Felicity's. 'Thank you!' she wept. 'For what you did. You saved our son.'

'How is he?' Felicity asked.

'Small, but very brave. The doctors say that he has a strong will, that he is a fighter. We have named him Karim.'

Felicity left her to rest then, glad to have visited. But it wasn't only because Bedra was tired that she chose not to linger.

'Helen!' She watched her colleague frown and turn round. 'Helen—it's me. Felicity.' She saw her friend's eyes finally widen in recognition.

'Thank goodness,' Helen said. 'I've been walking past the royal wing every break I get. What on *earth* is going on?'

'I don't know.'

They sat in a small annexe off the maternity ward, and nobody gave them a second glance.

The *abaya* provided anonymity, and Felicity was grateful for it.

'This is my last shift.' Helen shook her head helplessly. 'I leave for the UK tomorrow. I can tell your family…'

'I don't want to worry them.' Felicity's voice was shaken. She was relieved, almost, that the story was out, but guilty for her imposition on a friend and guilty as to how bad Karim's actions sounded when she repeated them. 'Things seem better now. He has said that I don't need to take the test.'

'If you're sure it's his, why don't you?'

'I am not risking my baby for a man who refuses to believe me. I don't know what is going on. He said today that I should return to the desert once the King's surgery is over—that it is better for the people if they don't know of me yet. I feel as if I am being hidden.'

'Can you talk to him about it?' Helen asked. 'Can you tell him how you feel?'

A bitter, mirthless laugh shot out of her lips,

and Helen gave her a sympathetic smile. 'I'm sorry. Of course you can't. I forget sometimes just how different it is here.'

'He's nothing like the man he was at home,' Felicity said. 'But sometimes...' Her voice trailed off as she recalled the tenderness of last night, but she was too muddled to think. 'I need to get away. I need to think. Maybe once the operation is over...'

'Has he taken your passport?'

'No.' Felicity shook her head. 'I don't think he was expecting to bring me back here to the palace, but I've checked and it's still there amongst my things. I have no money, though.' She laughed again. 'I have every luxury you could want, but no money. I can rustle up some back in England...'

'I cannot help you,' Helen said. 'If it ever came out, I could never return and work here again.'

'I understand.' Defeated, Felicity moved to stand. 'But thank you—thank you for listening.'

'Felicity, sit down,' Helen said. 'Tomorrow

is the King's operation. Everyone will be distracted. It is your only chance.'

'You said you couldn't help,' Felicity said. 'And I truly understand. I don't want to involve you.'

'You had no choice but to involve me, but it has to be kept quiet.' Helen eyes held hers. 'This conversation never happened. You need a suitcase; you need to look as if you are flying home for a family emergency.'

'To who?'

'To the people at the airport—when you buy your ticket.' It was Helen who stood now. 'I am coming in to say goodbye to everyone tomorrow. I'll leave a case here in the annexe at midday, with money in it. But please, Felicity, don't acknowledge me at the airport. They will watch CCTV if you get away.'

'I can't leave tomorrow.' Felicity shook her head at the impossibility. 'I'm not leaving Karim on the day his father has surgery.'

'I think you ought to…' Helen ran a nervous

hand through her hair. 'Felicity, I think you need to. Then you can sort things out. You have to think of the baby.'

'I *am* thinking of the baby. It deserves a father.'

'Is Jamal pregnant?' Helen's worried eyes met hers. 'I know it is wrong to ask, but surely you can trust me that it will go no further—*is* Jamal expecting a child?'

'No.' Felicity shook her head. Jamal had a trim figure, and only this morning she had wept quietly and told Felicity about her shame at not being able to give Hassan a son. She had said that she was glad and grateful that Felicity understood.

'There are rumours that she is,' Helen said.

'Then the rumours are wrong.'

'These are rumours that come from the palace.'

'But why would they…?' Her voice trailed off. A thought so vile it didn't bear thinking started to trickle in, and she blocked it.

'If Karim believes it is not his child…'

Helen gave a tight shrug. 'They need an heir, Felicity. These are turbulent times, and the people need to know there will be an heir.'

'No.' She refused to believe it of Karim—remembered his hands on her belly last night, tender hands that had cradled the life within. 'He said I didn't need to take the test last night. He said that…' She recalled his words, and then she recalled something else.

I would give anything not to be King.

Was that what Karim had meant? In the throes of near orgasm had he admitted his dark truth? That he would give away his own flesh and blood rather than be King?

Was *this* the man she had thought she loved?

'You'll lend me the money?' Felicity could hardly believe the strength in her voice or the plans that were being laid. 'You hardly know me.'

'I believe you, though,' Helen said. 'And your situation is impossible otherwise.' She gave her friend a pale smile. 'Try to talk to him tonight—try one last time to find out his plans. But don't get too upset. If he gets any indication you are planning to flee, then he'll be watching you like a hawk. And if you can't talk, if you can't work things out...' Helen gave her a quick hug. 'I'll see you in the UK.'

CHAPTER SEVENTEEN

THERE wasn't any time to talk.

When she returned to the royal wing Jamal and Hassan had left, and even though she felt as if she had been gone ages her absence did not seem to have been noticed.

Karim came out from speaking with the surgeon, and then they were driven back to the palace, where Ibrahim had just arrived.

He was far friendlier than the rest—more western in his ways—but the brothers all headed off to discuss their father and their country as the women sat and chatted, mainly in Arabic. On the rare occasion they did translate, it only upset Felicity more—because they all spoke beautiful English.

Really she might as well not be there. So she removed herself.

She lay in Karim's bed in the palace and pondered her future—wondered if she had so spectacularly misread him. Her hand moved down to her belly—it was definitely starting to swell now, and she truly loved it.

She loved her baby with a passion she had never anticipated.

Oh, all mothers loved their babies—even reluctant ones often wept with relief when they held their infant after birth. But now Felicity understood how a woman could lift a car if their child was trapped. She lay in awe at the surge of maternal instinct to save, to protect her child, that flooded her body.

When Karim came to bed he refused to talk. He had argued with his brothers, Karim said. There had been enough talk for today.

He removed her nightdress.

And she let him.

She let him make fast, urgent love to her. Still he moved her, still as he slid over her and deep inside her she could not believe Helen's words were true. That the man who was groaning her name, holding her so closely, begging her to come with him, could ever do that to their child.

Her orgasm was intense. She clung to him in the most intimate way possible—because she needed to believe *he* was real. And afterwards she lay beside him, tried to keep the fear from her voice, tried to make tender post-coital conversation, asking a question surely any mother-to-be would.

'What do you hope, Karim?' Felicity asked against his chest as he held her. 'What do you hope for our child?'

'Everything,' Karim answered. 'For our child, I hope for everything.'

His words brought no comfort—no comfort at all.

CHAPTER EIGHTEEN

KARIM needed to think.

His prayers were for his father this morning, that he might live. And not for selfish reasons either.

He wanted his father to have time—to amend the past, to meet again with the woman who had loved him even when she had strayed. Deeper into prayer he went, round and round in circles in his mind. He asked that he might forgive, that he might trust even if the answer wasn't the one he craved.

And for a surgeon that was hard. For a reluctant king it was harder.

He sat on the terrace and looked over to the

desert, handing over the control that he had always lived by.

She was pale, sipping on her tea, her eyes downcast and shy. How he wanted to confide in her—and yet he didn't want to cause her pain.

He did not want this, the greatest honour that could be bestowed upon him, and what Karim was now contemplating made him feel sick at the chaos it would create. Last night he had broached his plan to Hassan and a shouting match had ensued.

He stared out to the desert and felt its call. His last visit there had been dishonest. He must return and take counsel from the land, let it guide him to the right decision. Not just for himself, not just for his country. His eyes went to Felicity, to one woman versus a whole nation's hopes, and he was angry. He was angry because without her there would be no decision to make.

Without her, duty would be done so much more easily.

'Karim...' Her hand was shaking as she placed the tiny jewelled cup down. 'What you said last night...'

'Felicity,' he interrupted, 'today my father undergoes surgery...'

'What happens then?' she pleaded—because she had to be sure. Her last chance to leave was today, and she wanted his assurance, wanted the man who made love to her at night to return by day. She was too scared to trust him. 'Are we to have our wedding celebration? Am I to be announced to the people?'

'There is no time for discussion now,' Karim snapped. No one argued with him. No one except her. At every turn she challenged not just his words but his mind. 'Can we just get through today? And then...' He closed his eyes, made himself say it, forced the words out. 'I will tell you tonight.'

'Tell me what?'

He opened his eyes and she was still there.

Time was running out, and whether his father lived or died he had to tell her the truth. 'I will tell you everything.'

But she needed everything *now*—and there wasn't time. That much she understood.

A maid came in and announced that his brothers were ready to go to the hospital. Karim dismissed her before addressing his wife again. 'We will talk tonight. But I must leave now. Today I must show the country our family is strong. You will wait here.'

'I'm coming with you,' Felicity said. 'I want to be with you.'

He paused; he had always thought that he would have to face this day alone. This life, this pain was so much easier with her beside him.

'Very well.'

The maids slipped her *abaya* over her head, and as they were driven to the hospital Felicity's mind was in turmoil. Last night's assurances were so much sketchier by day. Still she had no idea of the fate that awaited her.

He had promised they would talk tonight—but what was it he wanted to tell her?

She had a voice, Felicity assured herself—with Karim, she had a voice.

Helen had surely got things wrong.

'Karim?'

He didn't even turn his head, just stared out of the window, completely immersed in his own thoughts. And of course she was ignored as they walked through the hospital and sat in the lavish lounge as the King was prepared for surgery. Hassan didn't look up as they entered and Jamal it seemed deliberately wasn't looking at her. The tension in the room was unbearable as the hour approached. Felicity was sure it wasn't just to do with the King. None of the brothers spoke or acknowledged each other. Even Ibrahim sat with his head in his hands.

It was an appalling, oppressive place to be, and Felicity was tempted to stand, to go for a walk—anything that would break the stifling silence. But then she felt something so strange, so unfamiliar and unexpected, it made her breath catch in her throat.

Karim's hand was in hers.

This strong man was holding on to her. And all Felicity knew was that today she couldn't go—couldn't add to his pain, to his grief. She knew that somehow she had to trust that beneath it all the Karim she loved was still there, and he would do the right thing. Her fingers gripped his. This display of affection was so out of place in this country, with this man, and it moved her.

'The King would like to speak with his sons.'

Hassan stood, looked over to Karim and spoke in Arabic. There was challenge in Hassan's voice as he spoke, but Karim didn't rise, just sat in stony silence.

Hassan went in first, and his face was like chalk when he came out.

And then it was Karim's turn. There was no emotion to be seen. When he returned his face was a mask, his back so straight. Felicity took his hand again. He needed her.

And then in went Ibrahim. He was there for a long time, and his eyes shot daggers at Karim when he came out. Karim didn't look up, just stared fixedly ahead, only jolting when Khan spoke again to his wife.

'The King wishes to speak with you, Sheikha Felicity.'

She felt his hand grip hers. Her eyes flew to his.

'I will come with you,' said Karim.

'He wishes to speak with the Sheikha alone.'

'I will come with her.' Karim stood up, but Khan shook his head. The King had given his orders. 'He insists on speaking to the Sheikha alone.'

Khan had told her how she must greet the King, saying that she must tell him she would pray for him and that he would be cured.

'Thank you.'

He was so much older than the images she had seen of him. Feeble and pale, he lay on the bed. The attentive nurses and his aide disappeared. His speech slurred slightly as he greeted her, and his eyes struggled to focus. No doubt, Felicity realised, from his pre-op medication.

'You are a good woman,' the King said. 'I can see that. Karim has told me that.'

'Thank you, Your Majesty.'

'You carry a great gift; you must take care of the baby.'

He *knew*! Her eyes whipped to his, to eyes as black as his son's, and she was touched that Karim had confided in his father. It was right he should die knowing of his grand-child's existence.

'I hope for a son.'

Felicity smiled. He did not mean to offend. She understood that much of their ways, at least.

'Our people need a son, an heir…' He was closing his eyes, then forcing them open, and Felicity felt the first prickles of confusion. 'They need to know that there will always be the King to guide them after I am gone. Hassan was raised to be King.' He smiled at her pale face. 'Karim would never say his first duty is not to his people—he would never say it. But I know he does not want to be King. This way, because of your gift, our people will get an heir and Karim can have the life he wants. I know Hassan will be a fine father to your infant.'

'Hassan?' She wanted to be sick. It was *true*! It was true and it had all been decided.

'When I close my eyes as they put me under I will pray for our future King…' He gave in to the drugs then, and Felicity just stood there. She wanted to shake the old man awake, demand to know what the hell he meant. Except she knew already. Full realisation was hitting her with devastating force.

This was not her baby to them. This was a solution.

This was what Karim was going to tell her tonight.

She stood frozen as the truth dawned bitterly. Karim had *told* her that he didn't want to be King. He hadn't been relenting, as she had thought. The results of the DNA test didn't matter—the baby she was carrying was a mere solution to them.

This was not a living, breathing child, but an heir to the throne—at whatever cost.

So *this* was what Karim had been planning: to hide her away until she gave birth. This was what he was going to tell her tonight.

This was the man she had thought she loved.

It was imperative that she leave—essential that she act completely normal as she walked out and joined Karim in the lounge.

'What did he say?' His question was low, but urgent. She saw the dart of worry in his eyes and knew he was worried what his father had said. Never had she been more grateful for the *abaya*. She only had to lie with her eyes. But still that was hard.

'To take care of you.'

'He said that?' Karim sounded surprised. 'What else?'

'Nothing…' She lowered her gaze. 'He fell asleep…the drugs…' She couldn't maintain normality, but for her child she *had* to—for the sake of her child she *had* to leave.

A few moments later the King was being wheeled to Theatre, and the clock-watching began. If a doctor appeared too soon then they'd know the operation had been hopeless.

There was a sliver of hope as an hour passed—but not for Felicity.

She stared at the clock, watched it inch past eleven-thirty. This was her chance.

'Karim…' She blew out a breath. 'I don't feel well. I feel a bit sick.'

He frowned at her strained, breathless voice. Felicity wasn't putting it on—her breathing was coming short and fast through fear, and she was so nauseous she felt she might really vomit. His concern was genuine, but Felicity realised it was for the baby rather than her. Karim told her he would summon a nurse, or a car would take her to the palace.

She shook her head. 'It's morning sickness. I might just have a walk in the gardens, like I did yesterday. It helped,' Felicity said. 'I want to be here to hear the news.'

'It could be hours…' Karim started, but Felicity halted him.

'If I need to go back to the palace I will get a driver to take me. You just worry for your father.' And he *was* distracted, Felicity thought as she walked away. Because usually she would be sent with an escort. Or perhaps after last night, he thought he had won her over…

He almost had.

Just as Helen had promised it would be, there was the case. Felicity opened it, grateful it was filled with clothes. It looked exactly as if someone had packed it in a hurry, and there too was a wad of cash.

Taking off her *abaya*, Felicity hung it on

the back of the door. Picking up the case, she walked out.

She was just another relative, just a blonde woman who turned a couple of heads, but there was nothing unusual in that, even though there were cameras set up outside the hospital, giving the people updates as the country prayed for its King.

She climbed into a taxi and asked to be taken to the airport. The driver started the engine. He was listening to the news, which, from the teeny bit she could make out, was about King Zaraq.

It *was* the right time to flee; the airline staff were all watching the news too, barely listening as Felicity explained that her sister was ill and that she *had* to get the next flight home.

She held her breath, wondering if her name would set off alarm bells, if Security would suddenly grab her. But then there was a ticket in her hand, and she was going through.

Cold sweat drenched her as her passport

was checked. At every stage she expected a hand to be placed on her shoulder.

There was Helen—their eyes met for a second, but Felicity quickly looked away. She sat tapping her foot, and faced the interminable wait for the flight to board.

If he rang, her heart would surely stop—because if she didn't answer it would cause alarm. And if she did he might hear the background noise of the airport. Armed guards were everywhere. She felt as if everyone was looking—as if everyone must know.

She tried to walk nonchalantly to the restrooms, then locked herself in a cubicle and waited the hour out. She stared at her phone. If he was going to call then it was better it was now. He called.

'Felicity?' It was almost a relief to hear his voice. Then there was a terrible struggle to remember her place, to be the suitable bride, not to ask but to be told. Only that wasn't her, and Karim would notice the change.

'How is he?' she asked—because that was what the old Felicity would have said. The old Felicity, who had cared.

'It is three hours now since they started.' She could hear the strain in his deep voice, but it didn't move her. Her hand over her stomach, she remembered what really mattered. 'How are *you*?' he asked.

'Tired,' Felicity said, staring at the wall in front of her and closing her eyes at the horror of it all. 'Just tired.'

There was a pause, an interminable pause, and then he spoke. 'Felicity, my—'

Whatever he was about to say was drowned by the flushing of the toilet in the next cubicle, which made Felicity's heart race. She tried to smother the phone. Instead of questions she got an apology—clearly he thought she was still feeling sick.

'I will go. You need your space. Try to rest. If you need anything…'

And as she said goodbye, as she clicked off

the phone, it was for all the world as if she had been speaking to a man who trusted in her.

But she was running away.

Even as the plane taxied down the runway, still she expected it to halt—for police or soldiers to flood the aircraft. Then they were in the sky; the seat belt sign was pinging off. Only then did it dawn on her.

She wasn't safe.

She could never be safe.

She had taken away their King.

CHAPTER NINETEEN

'ARE you okay?'

They were standing in the line for the plane's toilets when Helen first spoke to her.

'I feel sick,' Felicity admitted. 'I'm not sure if it's nerves or morning sickness.'

'You'll be home soon,' Helen said.

So would Karim. Maybe she was being paranoid, Felicity told herself as she locked herself in a cubicle. Maybe he would just accept that she had gone. After all, his mother had left…

And then her thought processes stopped. The red on her panties she had wished for in those early days was there now. And fear of Karim's wrath was nothing compared to the fear mingled with grief that hit her as she felt a low, cramping pain in her abdomen.

She was losing her baby. The very thing she had fled to protect was slipping away, and there was nothing she could do.

Nothing.

Helen frowned as her friend came out of the bathroom.

'What's wrong?'

'Nothing.' She didn't want to involve Helen.

'Felicity, there's something wrong; you're as pale as anything.'

'I'm bleeding.'

The staff were lovely. They moved her up to business class, where she could lie down, pulled curtains around her. But really there was nothing anybody could do. She stared out of the window as she slid through the sky, the cramp in her abdomen telling her nurse's brain this was real.

And she couldn't weep—because if she started she would never stop. She had to try and hold it together as the plane landed, then had to wait for everyone to offload so they could bring a stretcher on.

The case Helen had packed for her still had to be collected, Customs regulations still had be adhered to, but it was all dealt with efficiently and speedily.

She was in England. She was home.

An ambulance was waiting, and the paramedics told her to rest on the stretcher as they put in a drip because her blood pressure was low. Still she didn't cry.

It wasn't an emergency, the bleeding had stopped now, so there were no lights or sirens. Only with the airport out of sight did she dare to turn on her phone. Texts and voicemail messages bleeped, filling her inbox. In a matter of seconds it rang, and only then did Felicity fall apart.

'I lost it.' She hated him so much in that moment, she screamed her torment into the phone. 'I lost it on the plane. You can hate me and you can find me, but I don't care. I hate you, Karim. I hate you for never trusting me.'

CHAPTER TWENTY

FELICITY.

As he'd sat in the hospital awaiting news of his father still his mind had been on her.

She gave him strength.

A different sort of strength from the type he was used to. Holding her hand today had helped him.

The surgery had been long and delicate. For twelve hours the country had paused, and so too had Karim.

Refusing food, he'd drunk only water. Hassan hadn't been talking to him, Ibrahim had been immersed in his own thoughts, the aides and servants had stayed silent.

Oh, there had been many hours to think.

He'd rung her once, but she was resting, so he'd left her alone to do that. She would need all her strength for tonight, when he must tell her. Whatever the outcome, she had to know the plans that had been laid. How reckless he had been with their baby and the decision he had made.

Their baby.

It had been at the forefront of his mind even as he'd spoken with his father's surgeon. He hadn't spoken with his brothers or his aides. He'd walked out of the hospital with apparent dignity. Yet he had felt filthy inside. He'd wanted to fall into bed and into her arms instead of telling her the truth. But he wanted it out all the same.

But she was gone.

There was no fresh scent in the bedroom, no movement in the bed. Even as he demanded answers from Security, from his drivers, from the airport, even as all the accommodation at the university and the hospital complexes were checked, he knew that she was gone.

Every minute he rang her—and it nearly killed him when she finally answered.

His baby was gone. Before he had even acknowledged it. Before he'd had a chance to love it. Felicity too. They had both gone, never to return.

The news was confirmed by the airline. Yes, a Miss Felicity Anderson had suffered a miscarriage on the plane.

Except she was a sheikha, Princess Felicity Zaraq. Had he alerted them, had he kept her in the desert, maybe they would both still be here?

'It is probably better.' Hassan now spoke to him. 'She was weak. She would have revealed—'

It took Ibrahim's hand to block Karim's punch.

'I must go to her.'

'Why?' Hassan frowned. 'Our people need you here. You don't even know where she is.

She would be a fool to go straight home. Get security to trace her, and then you can decide her punishment.'

'She's just lost a baby.'

'It probably wasn't even yours.'

This time Ibrahim's block was too slow.

His mother was kinder, her voice at the end of the phone gentle and worried, and Karim knew she was speaking the truth.

'Is that what you really wanted for her? To keep her trapped in the desert or locked in your palace with the airport on alert? That is not how you love a woman. It is how you keep her, perhaps, but that is not love. Let her go, Karim. For two years I lived in fear of your father finding me. If you really love her, ring her or write to her and tell her that you are letting her go. Zaraq's ways are too different for some. I loved your father, I tried to fit in, but I couldn't. I am ashamed of what I did, but I was bored, unhappy. Your father was always in demand, myself always silent. Is this the life you want for the woman you love?'

'It would be different for Felicity. I would change.'

'Your father promised me the same.'

His mother's voice brought him the closest to tears he had ever been in his life.

'I am sorry you lost the baby.'

He had doubted Felicity and now he was paying the price. But there had been *so* many women, and never an accident. Karim dredged his memory bank, and as he sorted the blitz of emotions and feelings into slightly neater order he suddenly *knew*.

Opening his bedside drawer, he pulled out a condom, opened it and headed for the sink, filled it with water and watched its slow leak.

Leila. He remembered her jumping when he'd caught her in his bedroom, understood now her reluctance for anything oral. She had been damaging the condoms, procuring his seed, doing her best to ensure that the marriage he had been resisting would take place with her.

He just wished he'd worked it out earlier.

Wished he had had it in him to believe in Felicity sooner.

It would be easy to lie down now, to give in to tears, to follow all the advice. But that had never been Karim. Picking up the phone, he listened to his heart and summoned the royal jet.

CHAPTER TWENTY-ONE

THEY kept her in for two days.

As she lay there, Felicity decided to lie to her mother, to ring her as she had from the desert and pretend that she was fine. But mid-conversation she couldn't do it. She broke down. And even if her mother was anxious when she arrived at the hospital, even if Georgie was in tears, crying on a nurse, somehow it was worth the pain she had caused.

It was such a relief to be in her mother's arms.

Later, she took a call from Georgie at the flat, and answered calmly when she was informed there was a man called Karim at the door and Georgie asked should she call the police or let him in.

'Let him in,' Felicity said calmly. 'Tell Karim that when I am ready I will talk to him—you go to Mum's.'

Her eyes screwed closed as she hung up the phone. Even with freedom beckoning, still her mind searched for closure.

She went from the hospital to her mother, and let herself be looked after. She refused to call Karim, and he, as requested, did not call her. The waiting game they had played in the desert was being repeated again.

'Here.' Georgie brought her a tray laden with toast and scrambled eggs and a vast mug of tea. 'You're to finish it,' she instructed, and it was nice that finally it was Georgie telling Felicity this and not the other way around. As Felicity ate her lunch she glimpsed a future that was better—where the Anderson women were stronger—and knew that day was about to come.

But she had to deal with something first.

Stepping into her flat on day five, she was ready to face him.

He looked terrible.

Sitting on her sofa, wearing jeans and a T-shirt, he looked like a man who hadn't slept in a week. Or shaved, come to that.

'I'll never go back,' she said. She dropped her handbag on the floor next to Helen's case and told him, 'Nothing you can say will make me go back—you'd have to kill me first.'

'You really think I would do that?'

'I'd rather you didn't,' Felicity said. 'But, frankly, I'm so tired right now I actually don't care.'

'About the baby…'

'I *hate* what you were planning.' She watched him flinch. 'If you want to do your precious DNA test, if you need to check, then you still can—at the hospital.' She was talking as if she didn't care, except tears were rolling out her eyes and she spat out her words. 'It was *your* child—and you would have given it to Hassan rather than be King yourself.'

'No!' He was on his feet. 'When I thought it might be another man's, *then* we spoke of it…'

'Do you think that helps?' Felicity demanded. 'You would have done that to me—you would have ripped my baby from my arms and given it to your brother just so Zaraq had its heir.'

'I wouldn't have.'

'Your father told me your plans.'

'I wouldn't have,' Karim said again, his voice strangely calm. 'I thought I would. I thought I could. But, no. That night we were together, I knew that I could not.'

'Please,' Felicity scoffed. 'You told me you didn't want to be King—and without an heir, without *our* baby, Hassan couldn't be either.'

'No!' He demanded her attention, his black eyes fierce—not with anger, but with something she couldn't interpret. 'I did *not* want to be King. Have you any idea how hard that is to say? If I didn't hand over the baby Hassan would have stepped aside and I would have been King. It was my duty, it was my role and yet it was the last thing I wanted. And if it is the last thing that *I* want, how could I wish it for my son?'

And for the first time he cried.

'I did not want that future for him,' Karim explained. 'I did not want it because I knew what was coming—the burden that it would place not just on him but on you.'

She recalled her own words and realised how hard it would have been to hear them. Every cell in her body paused as he told her the truth.

'I told my brothers the night before my father's operation that the baby would stay with me. Hassan and Jamal were furious. They want to rule, they were bred and raised for it, yet I was denying them the chance. They kept telling me that it wasn't even mine…' He was silent for a moment. 'And I told them that even if it wasn't mine, I would rather love it than lose you.'

She turned to his proud face, looked at the tears that had dried on his cheeks, and prayed she would never have to see them again—would never see this proud man reduced by her doing.

'I told them too that I would not be King.'

'Then who?' Her mind darted, remembering the daggers Ibrahim had thrown at his brother. 'Ibrahim?'

'We did not know.' Karim shook his head. 'We chose to keep the decision from my father before surgery, but when he came round we told him what had happened.'

'He's alive?'

'He has many years left in him,' Karim said firmly. 'And Hassan has many years more.'

'Hassan?'

'He loves Jamal—that stuffed shirt of a guy actually does have feelings, and he loves Jamal. Even if she can't give him a son. Infertility happens to everyone—and if the people of Zaraq can't accept that yet, then there are many years left to educate them, to work out a solution.' His eyes met hers. 'To learn that there are other ways of doing things.'

And she wanted to believe, wanted to tell him so, but she was too tired to think straight, too tired to trust in her own heart.

The Sheikh, Prince Karim of Zaraq, would just have to learn patience.

'I'm tired, Karim.'

She slept in her own bed for a day and a night, and a day and a night more. She padded out occasionally, to the loo or the kitchen, and always he was there.

A sexy sheikh, topless in jeans, struggling to squeeze a teabag.

Once she had to smother a smile as she walked past and saw Karim on his knees, trying to work out how to change the loo roll.

He didn't really know what to say when she wept, so instead he just held her or, when she didn't want him, pushed a tissue under her bedroom door. And then, when she emerged from her room for longer intervals, he some-times patted the sofa and sat silent as they watched a movie.

And she healed a heart that was broken, because that was what women did.

There was a lot of healing still, but Felicity knew she was starting to get there one morning when she laughed at a silly joke he had made. And later that day when she glanced out of the window to smile at a daffodil.

She healed, and he let her do so at her own pace—until the third night, when she sat on the sofa beside him and he said those three words that she wasn't sure she was ready to hear.

'I love you.'

She stared at the TV screen, at her favour-ite soap, and wondered if they got it in Zaraq. Then she remembered who he was—a sheikh, a prince, a man who could do anything. Of course she'd get her programme. He had just given her his heart.

'I will stay here as long as you want me to.

I will stay here for ever if you will have me. I have duties and commitments, but they are nothing compared to my duty and commitment to you.' And then he said it again, but this time he added her name. 'I love you, Felicity.'

'Say it again.' Still she stared at the screen, the indecision that had plagued her these last days fading as over and over he said it.

'I love you… Felicity, I love you… I love you, Felicity.'

Every way possible he said it, and whatever road her mind darted down, he blocked it with his words.

And then she turned and faced him.

'So you should, given I'm your wife.' She accepted his nod, and then she said it, tears streaming down her cheeks as she let herself trust him. 'And given that I'm having your child.'

'You lost it.'

'No.'

'You told me…'

'I thought I had…' Felicity gulped. 'When I rang you, I truly thought I had.'

His eyes were stunned. 'You let me grieve. You let me think I'd lost my child!'

'Because you almost did,' Felicity said angrily, because it was essential that he see how close he had come to losing them both. As little as fifteen minutes ago, still she had had doubts, wondered if he was just saying and doing the right thing in order that the Prince could collect his wife. 'I had a placental abruption, like Bedra, only not as severe. I was told to rest and heal, told that there could be no stress if I wanted to hold on to my baby.'

He closed his eyes. He understood why she had done it to him after all he had put her through, could see why she had felt unable to tell him.

'When I was having the scan, and I realised the baby was alive, I promised her I would never go back, promised her that I would keep her safe. I promised her I would never let you know…'

'Her?'

It had never really crossed his mind that they might have a girl!

His hand moved to her belly, uninvited but very welcome.

'Meet your daughter.' She handed him the ultrasound photo from her purse, and watched as his face softened and a tender smile spread across that haughty face.

A smile reserved for the daughter who would unashamedly melt his heart and twist him around her little finger.

'I am perhaps the only royal prince who would rather have a daughter.'

And the sofa was too small, so despite the early hour he took her to bed, just so he could hold her properly. And he remembered the first time he had realised he might love her— the night when he had held her without lust—

and he closed his eyes in sweet relief as he did it again.

He held her close and relished that he could.

And because she should rest, because she was dozing, it was Karim who reached out and answered the phone, speaking for the first time to his mother-in-law. She wasn't anxious, as he'd expected, in fact she was very assured. She told him in no uncertain terms how she expected him to treat her daughter. Karim held the phone from his ear as Felicity lay half awake, smiling.

'Give me that.' She took the phone from Karim and spoke to her mother as he lay back on her rather small bed and stared up at her. His throat tightened when he heard her words. He was humbled at how far her love went.

'I really am, Mum—once the baby's a bit stronger…' She smiled at her man and he smiled back. 'I'm going to live in the Kingdom of Zaraq.'

EPILOGUE

'I CAN'T do this!' Jamal screamed.

And she might have been raised to be Queen one day, but Felicity and Dr Habib shared a hint of a smile as this very prim lady uttered a few choice words.

'I should be in the Royal Suite!' Jamal demanded.

'It's being painted,' Felicity soothed for the fiftieth time. 'For your baby's arrival!'

'Well, it's coming *now*,' Jamal said, her face darkening as she bore down.

Five weeks premature, the future King had caught Zaraq on the hop!

The suite wasn't being painted—that was a

midwife's lie—there had been a shift in the building and it had been closed off. But Jamal didn't need a long explanation. Jamal just needed to concentrate on the important task at hand.

Felicity had wanted to be there. In the past year or so she and Jamal had put aside their differences and become friends, and Felicity had been building up to asking if she could attend the birth. But babies came when they were ready—and this one had decided to make its entrance sooner rather than later.

Karim was in the middle of operating, Hassan was in the middle of a speech on the other side of Zaraq, and the King was over in London—as he seemed to be rather a lot these days. So not only was Felicity birthing coach, she was also shouting orders to Khan through the labour ward doors between contractions, telling him that Hassan must hurry if he wanted to see his child born.

'He is here!' Khan said excitedly.

'In a few more minutes he will be allowed in…' Dr Habib said, because traditionally males didn't enter till the very last moment.

But Jamal had other ideas.

'Hassan!' She screamed for her Prince, and who was Felicity to deny her? She invited Hassan in to share in the miracle of birth. And as cameras were set up at the entrance to the hospital, and people buzzed with rapid excitement, a strange peace filled the room as a baby was born.

Yes, he was destined to be a king. But as his mother scooped him into arms that had ached for ever, as Hassan wept and finally got to hold his son, he wasn't a king, he was something greater—a baby, a miracle. With tears in her eyes as the family entered, Felicity was grateful for the arm that wrapped around hers as she and Karim both remembered the day they'd first held their own gift.

'Georgie's got her outside,' Karim said, stroking his nephew's cheek and blinking for a moment, remembering little Kaliq and praying he was safe and loved too.

Georgie had come to help with her niece. Felicity didn't want a nanny, or a maid, she wanted her sister. And there was Azizah now, cooing and blowing bubbles in her auntie's arms. Felicity scooped her up, surprised at how heavy she felt after holding Jamal's baby.

They had chosen Azizah's name carefully. It meant precious and cherished, which she was every day. Both her parents knew what a true gift she was. It had been a difficulty pregnancy. Karim had refused to listen to her pleas to attempt a normal delivery, and after her Caesarean Dr Habib had told Felicity that her husband had been right.

They had both listened, and they both learned from the other.

Karim could be a prince and a surgeon too, so long as at home his only duty was to love her.

'Did I get here in time?' Ibrahim arrived,

neither present nor correct to meet the new King. He reeked of perfume, and Felicity smothered a smile as she spotted the smudge of a fresh bruise on his royal neck.

'Go and tidy up!' Karim growled to his younger brother, and Ibrahim walked off to do just that. Then Karim saw her pensive face and knew what was coming. 'Are you okay?'

'Fine. Can we talk?'

'Sure,' Karim said, although he wasn't.

'Could you watch Azizah? Karim and I want to go for a walk,' Felicity said to her sister, and then saw Georgie's pink face, and the rather wide eyes that lingered where Ibrahim had been. She had only been in the country for two days, and so far Felicity had managed to avoid them meeting, privately worried at the scandal those two might create. 'Don't even *think* about it.'

'I'm not,' Georgie said. 'Here—give me Azizah.'

They walked in silence to the gardens,

Karim in his navy theatre scrubs, Felicity in her pink maternity ones—just a nurse and a doctor walking and talking, a husband and wife enjoying each other's company, but also a prince and his princess too.

'You want to go back to midwifery.' It was Karim who broached the subject, and for that she was grateful.

'I enjoyed today so much. I knew I would. I've been looking forward to it.'

'You miss it?'

'Yes.' Felicity nodded. 'I didn't think I would. I mean, Azizah is three months old now, and I love spending time with her—I can't believe I want to go back to work. But maybe just one shift a week...' She turned troubled eyes to him. 'Is it impossible?'

A year ago the answer would have been yes, of course it was impossible. But times had changed since then.

He had listened to her, had let her lead him to his own conclusions and had told his father he could be both prince and surgeon. The news had been more acceptable, perhaps, because Jamal had announced she was pregnant…

He loved it.

He walked into the hospital in the morning and stretched his brain, and then came home to his family at night, which made his royal duties a doddle.

'Of course it is possible,' Karim said, hoping he'd catch his father in a good mood when he rang him in London tonight—though recently the King's mood had been excellent! 'Anything is possible,' he said firmly.

But his words didn't soothe her. Protocol Karim would take care of, but it was as wife and mother that she turned to him. 'Can I be all four?' she asked, and Felicity truly didn't know the answer. 'Sheikha, wife, mother, midwife?'

He took her by the hand and added to that list—tossed in a few balls more, knowing she would always juggle them. 'Sister, daughter, lover and friend…'

There was peace in his soul as he gazed down at her.

'Felicity, you can be anything you want to be.'

And she could…with Karim beside her.

MEDICAL™

Large Print

Titles for the next six months…

April

ITALIAN DOCTOR, DREAM PROPOSAL	Margaret McDonagh
WANTED: A FATHER FOR HER TWINS	Emily Forbes
BRIDE ON THE CHILDREN'S WARD	Lucy Clark
MARRIAGE REUNITED: BABY ON THE WAY	Sharon Archer
THE REBEL OF PENHALLY BAY	Caroline Anderson
MARRYING THE PLAYBOY DOCTOR	Laura Iding

May

COUNTRY MIDWIFE, CHRISTMAS BRIDE	Abigail Gordon
GREEK DOCTOR: ONE MAGICAL CHRISTMAS	Meredith Webber
HER BABY OUT OF THE BLUE	Alison Roberts
A DOCTOR, A NURSE: A CHRISTMAS BABY	Amy Andrews
SPANISH DOCTOR, PREGNANT MIDWIFE	Anne Fraser
EXPECTING A CHRISTMAS MIRACLE	Laura Iding

June

SNOWBOUND: MIRACLE MARRIAGE	Sarah Morgan
CHRISTMAS EVE: DOORSTEP DELIVERY	Sarah Morgan
HOT-SHOT DOC, CHRISTMAS BRIDE	Joanna Neil
CHRISTMAS AT RIVERCUT MANOR	Gill Sanderson
FALLING FOR THE PLAYBOY MILLIONAIRE	Kate Hardy
THE SURGEON'S NEW-YEAR WEDDING WISH	Laura Iding

MILLS & BOON®

MEDICAL™

Large Print

July

POSH DOC, SOCIETY WEDDING	Joanna Neil
THE DOCTOR'S REBEL KNIGHT	Melanie Milburne
A MOTHER FOR THE ITALIAN'S TWINS	Margaret McDonagh
THEIR BABY SURPRISE	Jennifer Taylor
NEW BOSS, NEW-YEAR BRIDE	Lucy Clark
GREEK DOCTOR CLAIMS HIS BRIDE	Margaret Barker

August

EMERGENCY: PARENTS NEEDED	Jessica Matthews
A BABY TO CARE FOR	Lucy Clark
PLAYBOY SURGEON, TOP-NOTCH DAD	Janice Lynn
ONE SUMMER IN SANTA FE	Molly Evans
ONE TINY MIRACLE…	Carol Marinelli
MIDWIFE IN A MILLION	Fiona McArthur

September

THE DOCTOR'S LOST-AND-FOUND BRIDE	Kate Hardy
MIRACLE: MARRIAGE REUNITED	Anne Fraser
A MOTHER FOR MATILDA	Amy Andrews
THE BOSS AND NURSE ALBRIGHT	Lynne Marshall
NEW SURGEON AT ASHVALE A&E	Joanna Neil
DESERT KING, DOCTOR DADDY	Meredith Webber

MILLS & BOON

millsandboon.co.uk Community

Join Us!

The Community is the perfect place to meet and chat to kindred spirits who love books and reading as much as you do, but it's also the place to:

- **Get the inside scoop from authors about their latest books**
- **Learn how to write a romance book with advice from our editors**
- **Help us to continue publishing the best in women's fiction**
- **Share your thoughts on the books we publish**
- **Befriend other users**

Forums: Interact with each other as well as authors, editors and a whole host of other users worldwide.

Blogs: Every registered community member has their own blog to tell the world what they're up to and what's on their mind.

Book Challenge: We're aiming to read 5,000 books and have joined forces with The Reading Agency in our inaugural Book Challenge.

Profile Page: Showcase yourself and keep a record of your recent community activity.

Social Networking: We've added buttons at the end of every post to share via digg, Facebook, Google, Yahoo, technorati and de.licio.us.

www.millsandboon.co.uk

0909/COMMUNITY LP